LOVE @ 13,500 ft

Deepanshu Saini

Published by:

F-2/16, Ansari Road, Daryaganj, New Delhi-110002
☎ 23240026, 23240027 • *Fax:* 011-23240028
Email: info@vspublishers.com

Branch : Hyderabad
5-1-707/1, Brij Bhawan (Beside Central Bank of India Lane)
Bank Street, Koti, Hyderabad - 500 095
☎ 040-24737290
E-mail: vspublishershyd@gmail.com

Follow us on:   

All books available at **www.vspublishers.com**

ISBN 978-93-815887-0-3
Edition: 2012

Printed at: Param Offseters, Okhla, New Delhi-110020

Dedicated to

My mom

Yu to zindagi ki raah me kai lehro ne seecha mujhe

Par vo thi teri hi kashti jisne mujhe doobne na diya......

(love u maa)

When we pray
God hears more than we say
He answers more than we ask
He gives more than we imagine
but
In his own time and in his own way

Acknowledgements

It will not be unfair to first of all thank GOD, who makes me what I wanted to be.

Anshuman and Sonal – I am very thankful to both of you for bearing me while I was writing this book. Very frankly, without you both this book wouldn't have been possible.

Sandeep Sir, for always motivating me for writing this book, thank you very much.

Vikas Shandilya Sir, thanks for all your well wishes and the time you spent for proofreading of this book.

Sonu bhai, my ideal brother; though it's true that I can never be like you, thanks for all those positive vibrations you always generate around me. Ritu Bhabhi - I am sure no one had tolerated my stories more than you, so thank you too.

There is still a *gang* that I would like to thank for a variety of reasons and I will name them now as I actually want to tell them how much they meant to my life. I thank – Ruchika (my sis), Ashu Bhai, Poonam Bhabhi, Sudhanshu Bhai, Mita Di, Abhijit Jiaji, Vipin Bhaiya, Rohit Bhaiya, Kavita Di, Manvi, Karan,

Sushma Di, Hemant Bhaiya, Saurabh, Gaurav, Sarthi, Noni, Ayan, Aaryan, Siya, Krish, Ishaan, Ravinder, Neeraj, Vinay, Ashok, Vipin, Mohit, Anuja, Ritu, Dev, Sanchayita, Paras, Neha, Swati, Rohit, Aakash, Inderjeet and I am sure many others whom I might have missed.

Special thanks to all those who made my trekking trip unforgettable – Partho, Nitin, Vivek, Sandeep, Anshu, Namit, Nishit, Pragati, Amandeep, Ankur, Shilpa, Manish, Swati, Shweta, Dwarka, Keshav, Ali.

Also big thanks to my publishers who trust me.

And finally but immensely, my dad, for being with me in my good or bad times.

Thank you very much.

Contents

Love always finds its way
but
If you love someone, just say.......

And the bottle stopped pointing towards Dhruv.

'Hey Dhruv, Truth or Dare,' Amandeep asked swiftly.

'Truth.'

'May I ask please,' Shilpa interrupted curiously. It seemed like she was waiting from a long time for the moment.

'Dhruv, please don't mind. But do you like Anjali?'

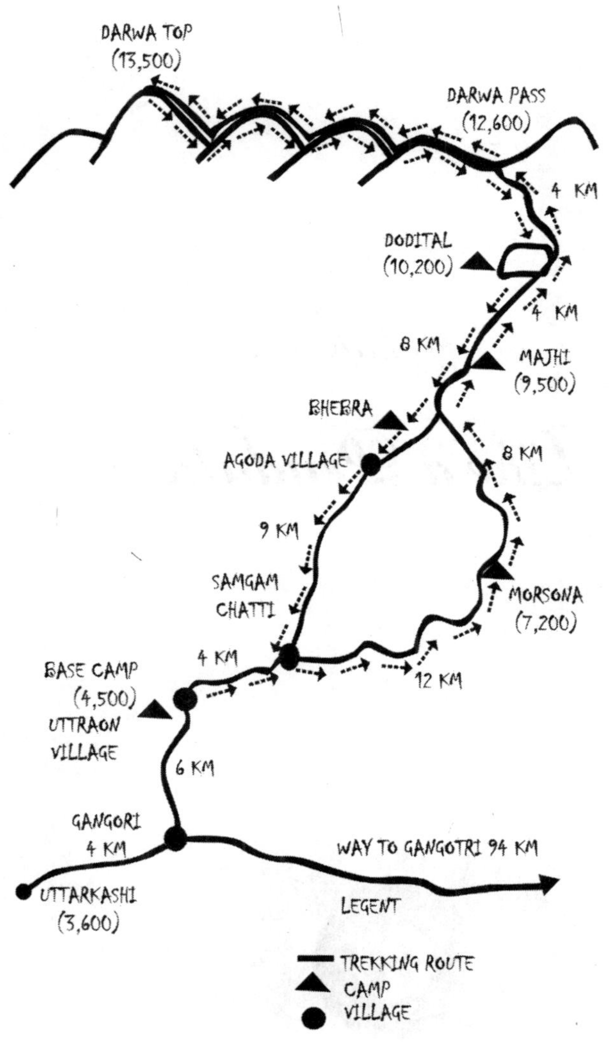
DARWA TOP
(13,500)
DARWA PASS
(12,600)
4 KM
DODITAL
(10,200)
4 KM
8 KM
MAJHI
(9,500)
BHEBRA
AGODA VILLAGE
8 KM
9 KM
SAMGAM
CHATTI
MORSONA
(7,200)
4 KM
BASE CAMP
(4,500)
UTTRAON
VILLAGE
12 KM
6 KM
GANGORI
4 KM
WAY TO GANGOTRI 94 KM
UTTARKASHI
(3,600)
LEGENT
TREKKING ROUTE
CAMP
VILLAGE

Chapter 1

Like a Pendulum

Sandeep swept through the door from his own cabin into mine.

'Finally, the News we were waiting for has come,' he announced brightly.

I raised my head from the file I was studying and shifted my brain into neutral.

'News... What News?'

'Mean you have not checked your Inbox till now.' He frowned and departs to pick up the phone that was ringing in his cabin.

Checking Inbox is one of the irritating works especially when more than half of the inbox had been filled by your boss's mails. I leaned back, massaging my neck muscles in order to concentrate directly on the desktop and clicked on the Inbox. It didn't take even a minute to me to understand the news, not news exactly; it was one of my dreams till then.

I smiled. The action was a relaxation in itself.

From:	Sahil.Kapoor
Sent:	Friday, October 27, 2010 12:43 PM
To:	Partho; Dhruv Gupta; Ankur Sangwan; Pramod Kumar; Amandeep; Deepak Kumar; Sonal Arora; Nitin Gautam; Sandeep Kumar Malik; Shweta Gabba; Swati Bhardwaj; Shilpa Nair; Manish Anand; Anjali Sharma; Dwarka Nath Murli; Pinaki Sarkar; Anshuman; Anshu Jayent; Nishit Sehgal; Namit; Vivek kaushik; Deepanshu Saini
Cc:	Suniti Sachdeva; Ashok Chauhan; Milli Gupta
Subject:	Outbound Leadership Training
Attachment:	Batch-1.xls; Batch-2.xls; Booklet.pdf; Batch-1.pdf; Batch-2.pdf

Dear All,

We are pleased to inform you that **Leadership course (Outdoor)** is being organised in two batches in the month of Nov/Dec 2010.

The Details are as under:

Program: Outbound Leadership Course

Dates: 12th Nov to 21th Nov and 6th Dec to 15th Dec 2010

Venue: Uttarkashi

Organising Agency: 'RUN D RISK' ADVENTURE FOUNDATION

You have been nominated to attend this program as per the enclosed list of batches.

Participation in this programme is compulsory for all trainees.

The Participants are required to reach the base camp at Uttarkashi on 11th Nov 2010 & 5th Dec 2010.

Accordingly you are required to depart from DELHI a day prior to the reporting date to Uttarkashi.

My name was listed in the Batch-2. The news made me filled with a sense of ecstasy and excitement; excitement to be away from work for so many days, excitement to be free from responsibilities, excitement to climb rocks, excitement to live in Jungles, excitement to trek 13,500 feet and excitement to be alone (*Important for me to come out from the memories of Shubhi*).

We were 32 people in total, going to Uttarkashi for a real fun or I must say – Adventure.

Oh! How can I forget? From the word Adventure, I must tell that somewhere I agree that the oldest and most widespread stories in the world are the stories of adventure and by then, the word for me was also like studied in books or newspapers and living it every minute, every hour and every day seemed to be very much excited. One could easily feel that excitement on my face, especially my parents who continuously had been observing me during the complete month of November. My heart was filled with emotion. The trip was actually important for me after the strain of last six months. It was the chance for me to be alone and I thought that it would help to heal the rift that was growing in my heart. I needed to build up myself again as it had taken such a bad knock since Shubhi left. So, I was in a hurry to go, though I admit that my clothes, medicines, camera and other important items were remained unpacked that very cool evening of departure – 5th Dec 2010. It seemed that now finally fear of love would be out of my system but I was unaware what God had actually written for me and I was ready with all my positive energy to welcome someone unwelcomed in my life.

'She will reach in ten minutes,' Swati said to Mr Rajesh, our team coordinator, a very gentle personality just sitting behind me.

It was about eleven at night, the driver was ready with the bus to take off. All were in excited mood, gossiping, listening to songs on their I-pods, having snap shots, calling their friends, relatives and other lovable. After all, in sixteen minutes, we will finally leave. Ten minutes for the arrival of her because of whom we were already late by half an hour, five minutes to place her luggage, and the last one for me to compose myself into the smiling and then have a warm nap.

Calling to Sandeep, I turned in to my seat, wishing fleetingly that at some point of time – just once would do – someone would enter my life with a happy smile and bring me some good news.

Sitting on my seat, I noticed absently that a girl was striding towards me, pink colour handbag swinging. Automatically, my brain shifted into an analytical mode, and I classified the footsteps. They belonged to a girl who had charted her own course in life and who knew exactly where she was going – and why.

Eyes to the ground, I pressed on, conscious that the time I had allocated for getting a nap was flying by.

'Is there something wrong?' A deep feminine voice brought me in present. The footsteps had ceased, their owner was addressing me.

I lifted my head and looked into the eyes that were like the sea below a clear sky, black and deep and fathomless. I went headlong into their depths, plunging, drowning, with as much chance of coming up for air as a diver floundering out of control.

Distractedly, my subconscious mind filled in the rest of her face. Her hairs were loose and straight, swinging nearly to the shoulders. Her face was narrow with sharp features. There was a short nose, the fine forehead, dimples forming the cheeks; attractive chin, the sensitive fullness of lips. Above all, there was the overpowering presence of a girl.

Those lips moved again. 'You look,' they were saying, 'as if you have the troubles of the entire population of the world on your shoulders.'

I surfaced, gasping for air, my lifeline reconnected. I broke into a laugh.

Shaking my head, my thick black hair swinging, 'Not the entire population, only a very small section of it,' I answered with an improper wink.

'Idiot' glancing at her watch, she moved further while pressing some numbers on her mobile.

At the turn, I glanced back. She was walking as if she had only just resumed her journey. Oh, yes, she knew where she was going. And, by the proud angle of her head, I judged that she would surely go there, on the last seat that was vacant, so that she could hang up on mobile.

Sandeep was continuously staring at me. Coming closer to my ears he commented, 'Sweet, beautiful and sexy?'

'With the most beautiful eyes you could hope to see in a girl', I said.

He was still staring at me, maybe in order to tease me, as such I was dying for her.

'No, never, never think of this. Me and love – not possible now.'

'What do you mean by Now?'

'Oh! Nothing. I am just saying leave her topic. Some girls make a grab.'

'Is that so?' Sandeep laughed, unbelieving it easily, 'But maybe you are interested to know her name.' He again stared at me with a smile and all of a sudden we started laughing.

Our laughter filled the bus.

'Anjali' That was her name, I heard along with the noise of horn, that driver *Mohan Lal* pressed while manipulating the thrust of an engine in order to leave the busy crowded roads of Delhi. I stared through the window to the dark night which beautified the approach to the large modern buildings. It seemed that now, I, having got the desertion of my ex-girlfriend out of my brain. My relationship has taught me a few things – the sad things actually and her memories were still fresh in my mind. I wished I could turn back the clock and begin my journey where everything ends.

Two arms came around me and smoothened cheek rubbed against mine. Replacing herself, she turned slowly into my arms and tears came then, the reaction to her quarrel with me, to her uncertainty as to whether she was doing right in wanting to stay away from me, the tug inside of the child she was intending to deny the guy she loved so deeply, when I wanted her so much.

'Take Care' – that were the last words she said while placing the letter in my hand.

The mobile ring thrust a misplaced trill into the atmosphere and I came out from her pull. I didn't really feel like receiving any call, but I wasn't ready to let my mood ruin the time for Shubhi.

Well, I hoped with a faint sigh that was the one problem that would not knock on my door now, pleading to be solved. If I still suffered from a residue of despair, or even badly battered psyche, I will try to battle with it with the positive energy that was somewhere taking birth in my soul. I would hardly seek out any comforting shoulder, I was sure.

'Maybe I was just kidding with myself. But as far as I was concerned, though, things couldn't have been worse,' I thought.

Mohan Lal just kept driving, staring at the moonlit road through the fog. Five hours passed in silence and I found it torture, really. I lowered the book I had been reading and looked around. Everyone was sleeping, just inversely proportional to my thoughts regarding cool introduction of all along with lots of gossiping and chattering. Why were all quiet, sleeping like they have never slept for last several years? What kind of people was I encountering out here? How far along will they go like this? The thought swirled around my mind and in order to dull that thought I decided to take snapshots of all while they were busy in their jobs. It's not less than any fun when you catch the people while they were sleeping, especially in the bus.

'So, it will be fun and it will be a challenge too,' I thought.

'Beautiful' for a few moments, I stood there, admiring her from the lens of my camera with something near to adoration on her face.

She was really beautiful. Oh! God! I forgot her name. Oh! Yes -Anjali. That was the name Sandeep told me.

Her eyes were closed and her hand tightened into a fist. It was a simple face, open and innocent, distant as the moon. She actually seemed to be blessed: courage, kindness, intelligence and grace. Her eyes were not less than any pearl. A strange expression passed over her face as such in a dream she was scolding someone. Then as she couldn't help herself, she tried to adjust herself in small available space between two seats. My heartbeats were racing. She was pulling me like a magnet but somewhere a voice inside was saying 'I must keep a distance from her. I don't want to strike once again by the girl's detachment.'

What if an instant voice kept trying to say 'I should get to know her.' I don't want my heart to be gambled like this, so I kept all my feelings battened down and drifted to the neighboring seat to have more snapshots.

The job went on for few more minutes and I stared out again at the darkening landscape, the shadowy trees receding in the way and the descending night. But it was becoming almost impossible not to remember the expression of Anjali's face when she had walked in the bus and while she was sleeping. Gradually, like always, the time passed and I spent it thinking about Anjali, Shubhi with no doubt and as well while listening to songs, reading books and taking some funny snap shots.

Sunlight streamed through the windows overlooking an open sky. A few stunted pine trees clung to the rocks. I engaged myself observing the vehicles passing by and was amazed to see so many at this hour of the day, although the traffic flow was wearisome. It was good to observe small hills. They looked dull and dark, no different from any of the other I had ever seen. But I had seen the value; the sparkle of sun rays was making them more beautiful.

It was also good to know that all were finally awake but seemed very much shattered. I could hear some gossips just like where we are? When will we reach Uttarkashi?

Even I was not surprised when semi-conscious, half-opened eyed Sandeep banged same question in my ears. I didn't reply as I was also unaware of the location. What I knew that the cold breeze outside my window was singing and dancing as such it was enjoying its freedom to the fullest. I could feel the freshness and simplicity of the area as such some positive force was heaving me towards it. Strangely, it seemed to me like someone was calling me, there was something that was tugging me, holding me completely.

And it was when Mohan Lal rode down the bridge, after evading through some fog, we came to know where actually we were and with sanctified mantras – *Har Har Gange!* (used to worship River Ganga in India) that released from my heart, I bowed my head to the graceful holy Ganges.

It was almost six and half hours after leaving Delhi, the bus stopped to the *Gateway to God* – Haridwar; the place where River Ganges descends to the plain from its source at *Gaumukh* at the edge of Gangotri Glacier. According to Hindu mythology, Haridwar along with *Ujjain*, *Nasik* and *Allahabad* is one of four sites where drops of *Amrit*, the elixir of immortality, accidentally spilled over from the pitcher while being carried by the celestial bird *Garuda*. The place is really a paradise for nature lovers. I was exhausted, and it felt good to stop and I am sure, same was the feeling of all others as all tiredness seemed to be flown away while approaching into the grip of sacred Ganga. Digging through my bag, I pulled out my travel kit I had made before leaving home; after all it was the time to freshen ourselves.

'Shall we need to change our clothes after taking a bath,' Dwarka asked while we stepped down from the bus. Fortunately, I should call him by his full name. Dwarka Nath Murli, the guy without whom the trip may seem to be actually boring, short, small headed with sweeping planes forming the cheeks along with stubborn chin. It was he, with a very bad sense of humour.

I preferred not to answer his stupid question and seemed to be lost in my thoughts. Stepping down the bus, I glanced across the open land with small shops in a row at side. It was very cold; temperature may be around 15 to 20 degrees.

'Hey tell! Will you change the clothes after taking bath?' Dwarka asked again while caressing his hairs smoothly.

'Fuck your thoughts,' I said. 'How could you think of having bath in such a cold? You will get freeze.'

'You are a black sheep.'

'You just do your job, massage your body with ointment; any girl would call you anytime.'

'Will they?'

'Yes,' I said.

Well I saw him adjusting his jacket properly. A way he has of holding himself and a certain glow in his eyes as if he was meeting his dream girl.

'God' I just hammered my forehead and moved from there.

Two and half hours were given to us by Mr Rajesh for bathing, breakfast and temple visits. And I am very proud to say that I did nothing among these. Bath – Never; you very well know the reason. Food; I mostly not prefer while travelling, especially the mountains; and temple, not because I don't believe in God, but because I don't believe in statue worship. So open-heartedly, I just clean my face and legs from the frosty Ganges water in order to wash away my sins, though I was not sure that all could be washed away.

Oscar Wilde, an Irish writer once said: "There is no sin except stupidity". So, is it a sin or stupidity to make some lovable cried? Is it a sin or stupidity to be indifferent to them who love you? Maybe it is stupidity but up to an extent, it is also a sin. May Mother Ganga will forgive me for this.

I drew into the deep breath. My body was normal but frostiness of water froze my heart. I was lost in my thoughts and travelled my times of yore in one single shot. You may think that I was sad for Shubhi, but that's not true. I had been angry at first, refusing to accept her decision of getting apart. But as I calmed down, I declared her 'I want us to meet again sometime, talk it over, and see how you feel then.' But I was sure she had, deep down, accepted that for a long time our relationship had really had nowhere to go.

Moving past the stairs descending to one of the ghats, where no tourist congregates to perform ritualistic bath, I just sat down. It was very peaceful to be there. I was very quiet but that was the only thing I was not interested in doing. Positively, I was not there to remember my past and get worried. I spent so many nights awake, wondering: How had the affair ended? Who had ended it? Where had she gone alone? Had she loved me more than I did? A six-month-long time of darkness and despair. But now, I also wanted to make new friends. I also wanted to sing songs, to dance, to enjoy the trip. After all, why should I get bothered about the person who was not bothered about me?

It was about a few weeks ago; I stayed for about a week in my uncle's house. There was a servant named Gopal, who always seemed to be happy, full of good humour. I asked him the secret behind his happiness, though he was so poor.

'Happiness never thinks either you are rich or poor when it knocks on your door *Sahib Ji*. It's only a habit with me to be happy,' he replied. 'Every morning when I awaken and every night before I go to sleep, I thank God for such a wonderful life.'

Gopal had made a practice of this regularly and became usual to happiness. He desired to be happy and succeeded. Similarly, I decided to be the same. My mind moves from the thought to the thing. I spread my arms to the fullest and took a deep breath as such Mother Ganga was teaching me to be lively, energetic and full of life. 'I deserve to be happy' this contemplation then accompanied me by a feeling of joy and restfulness in foreseeing the freedom of some burden from my heart as such I was flowing smoothly with the water. I found the new source of positive energy in me and remembering that the thankful heart is always close to the riches of universe I thanked god for those minutes that I spent happily with the love of my life. I pictured the fulfillment of my desire and feet its reality and experienced the joy of the answered prayer. It was really amazing to feel certain waves of happiness generated in my heart by the glory of Goddess Ganga. So, I was happy, happy for both me and Shubhi as I knew that her best is to be away from me and she could lead her life peacefully only when I will be away from her. And it was really good to feel like this, I examined truthfully when touching voice of some song drifted from somewhere.

'It's my kind of music,' I remarked appreciatively, and moved my feet to the direction from where the flowing sound course to me. It was a group of some girls bathing in a river and a mobile phone was tuning at one step of the stairs or rather I should correct myself by saying that there were the girls of our group listening to one of the romantic songs in Sonu Nigam's voice while bathing in the river.

'I think,' with a squashy smile, I eased away, 'I must put a distance from them, otherwise it could be hard for me.'

Hand-in-hand they went inside, holding each other, utterly shivering. It seemed that few mermaids had appeared together on the surface. All were looking stunning but my eyes were fixed on one. She was really gorgeous. Her pearl-like-eyes were huge now while chills shivered. I could feel her soft skin through her blue Reebok T-shirt with '*Guys Stay Away*' in bold white letters and her long-but-very-slim legs clothed with black shady jeans. Truly admit, a minute ago, I was in the hold of Goddess Ganga and now it seemed that the beauty of Ganga appeared itself on its surface. She really seemed to be god's real architecture. I never saw any girl bathing so skillfully in my entire life. My heartbeats battled, eyes got burned, seeking a path to the very heart of her, but skillfully I controlled my desires in view of the fact that I don't want to be the cause of any more tears now and consequently, in order to avoid the irresistible trap of her prettiness, I returned.

It was much better when I reached into the bus. I felt my soul happy and in order to celebrate the moment, I removed my jacket, throwing it aside as if it weighed heavily on my shoulders and speak out loudly the words, I was holding since last night.

'When we set out to do any kind of work, we approach the hurdles in the work with a known familiar ways or some skillful methods. These methods must be learned or studied. In the same way, there are accepted methods or skills for governing and directing our life, necessary to survive capably and happily. These methods are very important in our life. So, my dear friends can we all have a small introduction in order to reduce the distance between us to some point.' I smiled.

For a moment everyone got quiet but at the very next moment a heavy laughter of all led by Anjali amplified my smile. The sound of her laugh filled the day with its appealing richness and she smiled as an appreciation. I could also hear the appreciating noise of clap from someone sitting on the second last corner seat at my right and I understood that I can continue my conversation.

'Hello everyone, I am Dhruv Gupta from Delhi, working as an electrical engineer in Projects Deptt. I joined this company some four months ago. My hobbies are drawing, poetry, reading books and many more. Mr Paulo Coelho is my favourite writer and in one word I consider myself MAD.'

So this was my short introduction and I took my seat so as to hear the voices around me as likewise in the mean time, everyone introduced themselves, aware of the River Ganges that we had already left behind in the plains. Our elite party consisted of only bachelors, mostly excited like me. So, following the small introduction section, many strangers to each other got listed into the category of known and this was how I came to know that Anjali works in the finance Deptt. She loves to play badminton and Volley ball. Moreover, she loves singing songs, watching movies and shopping. Her sweet voice was still echoing in my mind since I heard it the day before.

I could feel the air of excitement around me. Putting my knees discreetly together and holding my back straight against the natural pull of seat, I sat down. Yet when the end of introduction came I could not help being eager by chatting with so many friends I had made. I was enjoying a greater freedom than I have ever known. I realised that my happiness resides somewhere in me only and it's my duty to hunt it out.

The train line ran along some way and disappeared. The beautiful hills rose majestically over the shimmering vast water of river Ganges, their sharp peaks already lost in the cold grey mists that were rolling down over the craggy brown hills. Everything was beautiful. Mohan Lal released the pressure on the accelerator and the bus slowed down to take some sharp turns in the way. It passed through villages, fields and valleys. Train line appeared again between the river and bay range. When the train passed from there, its noise could be heard all through the valley. You know, whenever I heard the sound of a train, I imagined me and Shubhi aboard it. I imagined us singing, dancing, travelling to the end of the world, seeing beautiful places.

Wow! An answer to my prayer had come. Now, my mind was receiving happy and positive vibrations. Up to some degree I was successful in bringing forth the highest and best in myself. Natural smile tugged at the corners of my mouth. I was actually happy and smile on my face enhanced more as I noticed the wide blue coloured board carved with 'WELCOME TO UTTARKASHI' in white, but I was aware of the fact that our destination or I must say, our base camp was still six to seven hours away from the point. So, where all were in the high spirits, busy in gossips and fun, my eyes were in position to shut down. After all, I had not slept for almost twenty hours.

All sounds seemed to be decreasing, light was just like moving away from my eyes, mountains seemed to be disappeared and lastly a shawl packed down on my face. Positioning myself to window pane, I eased my head sideways so that it could rest diagonally to the corner of the seat.

I dreamed that I was standing in the centre of road. Fairly heavy, the traffic was composed of an assortment of travellers on bicycles, motor-cycles, cars, buses and even men pulling carts laden with goods. Somehow the scene was pathetic and gloomy, with the figures seeming to blend in the falling rain. I was wearing my new dress that my only younger sister gifted me on my birthday. Meanwhile, Anjali was approaching me, having her handbag swinging in her hand, her hairs falling smoothly on her shoulders.

As I was waiting for her, I saw Shubhi coming towards me from another side. She called out me but her voice was not clear, maybe because the traffic was moving so loudly. Once she was gone, the image of Shubhi was replaced with a giant truck. I was supposed to get struck at my place. My eyes got broad with fear on my face. I was tattered into pieces.

The truck came closer and closer. I was sure I was going to squash, but what was this, at last second I felt Anjali's arm encircling my waist.

And I woke up suddenly with the push of Sandeep shaking me to bring back to my conscious mind while the dream was shaking me in sub-conscious state.

My mother once told me that all dreams are meaningful. It's our subconscious mind which tried to convey us some message through dreams. If we put ourselves in our dream and view the dream from that point of view, we can interpret whatever our dream wants to tell us. I tried to do the same with my dream, but I just came up with a mass of confusion. I was not less than any pendulum swinging back and forth continuously, sometimes to Shubhi and sometimes to Anjali. Really, it was like any puzzle to be solved.

'Hey Dhruv, we have reached.' Sandeep's voice came to my ears again. I rubbed my eyes and tried to see the surroundings. It was very dark. There seemed to be no light whatsoever. Even though, I was succeeded in passing seven hectic hours of travelling calmly, I was feeling very hungry. I tried to open the window for a while but a feeling of almost chilly air compelled me to lock it again.

Everything seemed to be traumatised. All were struggling to get down from the bus handling their luggage one by one. I pulled out the warm fabric, a woolen cap and a torch from my bag in order to be safe in every aspect. It seemed that my heart would burst out of my chest as I came out of the bus. Temperature had already fallen down beyond its limits. Almost nothing was visible except large number of stars twinkling over our head and about thirty lighted speck of torches in search of the way to the base camp. I could hear the noise of river flowing somewhere nearby along with lots of gossiping among all as such they were known to each other from several years. An excitement could be felt in every voice and every step. The world seemed different here than anywhere else.

So finally my life had reached to one of its dreams or rather I should say that my life was away from my ex-dream.

'Oh! No. I should only think about positive vibrations. Yes, only about the happy time I lived. I have to tell myself that I am overreacting. I have to stay positive.' I thought while a healthy tall man, not clearly visible, came from somewhere behind the bushes and instructed us to follow him and like mules following their master we followed others up the steps. It was quite tough to walk. Up and down the narrow path we travelled, twisting, turning, and easing over the torturous route, I saw big rocks at many places, river flowing beneath the bridge we crossed, large mountains surrounding us and the bulbs glowing at some distance. I cannot describe what relief I felt on crossing that bridge. As I was approaching towards the bulb, I felt that some strong power was pulling me towards it as such it would decide my fate. All weighty topics seemed to have slipped into the river and washed away with the rapids. The peaceful environment made me feel that everything was on right track – I was on the right track and it was after another ten minutes of walk, inching forward slowly with our luggage on our back, we reached to the base camp.

I felt excited beating of my heart as I entered the area. The place was nice, as I remembered. They had pitched the tents just hundred steps aside the river, small bulbs were glowing in each. I felt drawn to this place. It was cold and frozen. White stars were brilliant in the sky caught in the branches of moonlight. I smiled with joy and paused to gaze off instructors. All seemed to be energetic along with a young woman who saw me lost in my thoughts. Her name was Ms Poonam. I was struck by her appearance. She wore a plain black dress and a jacket. Her face was pale and bland, without a single touch of lipstick or other make-up. Her manner, too, was subdued yet somehow watchful, as if she imagined that those around her might suddenly start acting in an outrageous way.

'Hey, are you listening?' Leading instructor Mr Sandeep Sood asked me. So, here I will use Mr Sood in order to represent our instructor so as not to create any confusion between my friend Sandeep and our most handsome and well-built Instructor Mr Sood. He was in the middle of giving us a run-through of terms in order to prepare ourselves for our first lesson in the program.

I glimpsed the faces around me hesitantly. 'Uh, yeah. You were saying something about Rucksack'.

He shook his head. 'Right, I was talking about Rucksack. Rucksack is the thing used for carrying heavy loads, because of the limited capacity to carry heavy weights for long periods of time in the hands. So first keep your luggage in your tents and then collect your Rucksacks and other items one by one.'

Everything traumatised again. Everyone moved to keep their luggage. Two tents were provided to boys and one, obviously, for the girls. Activity to collect Rucksack and other items like tiffin, sleeping bags and warm inners goes on for around half an hour and a session of instructions carried out again after the dinner provided. We were sitting on small rocks, feasting on dinner of *rice*, *dal* and *chapattis.* The sky was thick with stars as usual. Aside from a few not-so-minor details, life was both terrific and terrible.

'What?' This is the word came out automatically from our mouths when we heard five main instructions of the night.

- ✓ You must get ready by 06:00 AM in the morning for a tea. It will only be provided up to 06:20 AM.
- ✓ At 07:00 AM we will leave for an exercise and jogging up to one km.
- ✓ No hot water will be provided for bathing. If anyone interested for a bath, he/she is allowed to have cold chilly water of river Ganges. (*It means I was not bathing for ten days. Yuck!*)
- ✓ Toilets for girls and boys are provided with water tanks nearby. So, every evening as a team activity, all have to fill the tanks.
- ✓ Another tank is provided near the river for washing the utensils after eating, also to be filled by all of you only.

'So, please get ready for washing your utensils now. Rest, we will interact tomorrow.' Sood sir ended firmly.

All moved towards the river. Water seemed to be flown more than its actual speed. It was actually very chilly. My hands got frozen for a moment.

'If you can hang on your hands for all thirty seconds in the water, your mission will be clear.' A known feminine voice with a tag of smile on her face responded me. Ya! You are right – that's Anjali.

'Oh! Hi,' I replied. 'What are you doing here?'

'You know.'

'Oops, sorry for a silly question, I remarked. 'Obviously, you are here to do the same thing I am trying to do.'

'Not exactly.'

'Mean?' I questioned while rubbing my hand on the plate.

'I want to apologise.'

'For?' Lines of confusion appeared on my forehead.

'For, what I said you yesterday night,' she said very softly.

'Oh! for baptising me as an Idiot.'

'Ya! Sorry for that.'

'And if I do not forgive you!' I was in a mood. I was almost giddy with excitement over something.

'Mean?' She asked in very low tone while raising her eyebrows. I could feel perplexion on her face. Do all girls are like this only. I didn't understand till now why they take some much tension for such stupid topics. But I should also admit that she was definitely cute. I could see the curiosity glittering in her eyes, the eyes that were arresting me. She wanted to know what I was going to say as much as I wanted to say it.

'Mean, you are very beautiful,' I said while pulling my jacket around my body and returned in the direction of camp. Before leaving, I could see both shy and smile on her face. I don't know what she was thinking that time but I was sure that she got relaxed. She understood that I was not angry on her. I expected her to follow me up to the camp. With our torches in our hand, it seemed to be like some detectives, searching for a clue to solve any mystery.

I turned my gaze back to her. Yes, she was some twenty steps behind me with Swati, Anshu and Shweta. Seriously, introduction proved very beneficial in order to remember the names of girl, especially.

Finally all finished the task and got busy in their work. Everything settled down. A long chain of twenty boys was formed from river to toilets and tanks got filled. All equipment already issued. Beds had been set. Lights got off and I was surprised to see the time. It was only nine. I have never slept so early. So, while all were packed in their sleeping bags, I decided to search the place.

It was after dusk, mountains get more frozen and stars start doing their job beautifully. Constellation could be seen with naked eyes. And same was the scene my eyes were encountering not for the first time. Temperature had dropped significantly.

Ready to move out, I focused my torch to different places. There she was, wide awake – huddled along the floor by the fire, arms wrapped around her knees. So, now, seeing her so soon, I hesitated to interrupt her loneliness though I wanted to hold her. I could feel something deep in my heart. Her hairs hung over her face, but from the way her shoulders were shaking; I could see she was shivering.

Wanting to help her, I offered her my jacket and at that moment our eyes met.

'No thanks,' she replied.

'As you wish. So, where are all other girls?' I continued with a small gap.

'They have slept.'

'And you didn't.'

'I don't sleep so early.'

'Did the loneliness bother you?'

'I am not alone. We are seven girls.'

'Ya! I know that, but that's their physical presence. Mentally, you are alone.'

'What do you want to say?' She questioned while rubbing her hands solidly.

'That you are alone.'

'It's nothing like that.' I noticed her pleasant features and easy smile.

'Okay.'

We said nothing for some time. Fire was reducing slowly and it felt to be more shivering so I kept on some more woods to maintain the temperature for a few more minutes. Wind blew down making the flame jump. I wished for the tenth time that time would pass like this only – she sitting in front of me and air lifting her hairs. Her eyes were intense as I stared into them. I wanted to kiss her. Memories of Shubhi seemed to be flown away somewhere for the time being and that was the only thing I wanted, but not like this to be replaced by another girl. I knew I should stop me but my brain had floated somewhere far away from my head. Kind of magnetism in her was pulling me. I turned my head a fraction of an inch in order to see her face clearly but I think she judged my movement.

'What happen?' Soft lips moved again.

'N...Nothing' I said. 'Just wanted to say Goodnight,' I continued.

'Goodnight!' She passed a sweet smile which made me think for a long time that she just likes me very much. But then I realised that maybe that's just the way certain girls are. I've noticed that a lot of time the girls who smiles at you the most are the ones who ended up like 'we are only friends dear.'

'I think I should also sleep now,' she continued and moved towards her tent while I was watching her in the hope that she will revert and say goodbye as happen in movies. Ya, I know that you will say that it's not a film, its real life buddy. But I must tell you my friend that she did. Yes, she reverted and gestured me 'bye' with a very sweet smile. God, I missed having her in my arms, but I doubted that she understood that I like her.

Everyone was packed in their sleeping bags with an alarm at 05:30 AM. I did the same but sleep didn't come along my ways for almost two more hours. I was now being attracted towards another girl, who was honest, sincere, loyal, faithful, and peaceful. These qualities that I admire were sinking down into my heart. The words of my mother echoed in my mind – Do not wonder how, why or where you will meet the mate you are praying for. Trust implicitly the wisdom of your heart. It has the power to carry out its mission. You don't have to assist it.

I salute the words. If she is right; if Anjali is my only mate then she will definitely be mine and if someone else is there, then she will automatically be on my way. So, I left everything on wisdom of my heart. I realised that this is – theoretically at last – a two way conversation. After all, Love is what love does.

I want everything to be positive and my mind to be free. So, I just closed my eyes, let go, relax the body, and became very quiet, passive and receptive. I reminded myself that I want to be happy and thanked God for such a beautiful life before I slept down.

As difficult it was to get stable in the sleeping bags, more difficult was to come out of it, especially when a sudden cold frozen wind smashed on your face. More torturous was the moment when you had to wash your face, brush your teeth and last, but not the least, when you strike an icy water on your butt early morning.

Just before the dawn, it was still very cold and iced up. My body was quaking even after wearing six clothes. Only two or three people were found to be lined up for tea but slowly many sleepy faces came into the view. Morning tea did good job for warming the body and then process of getting ready for an exercise started. Slowly, sunlight appeared like a magic and view started appearing clearly. I glanced from left to right. It was awesome. We were surrounded by majestically high mountains, stream of the river flowing generously in between. Ground was covered by a thin layer of mist. Long pine trees were stunted all around. Area was enchanting, trapped as it was between earth and sky in a mist of fog and fluttering clouds. Everything was natural. The snowy clouds rested on the ragged mountain tops, giving the area a picture-pretty beauty. 'I was dying to see such a natural beauty since I was a little boy,' I thought while we jogged. A single mile actually felt very long. I kept my company, moving parallely in two straight lines. The small radio in Sood Sir's hand was playing a local Garhwali song, which possibly favoured love. Perhaps he was thinking about someone lovable, but his mind was in the command of jogging, inner compulsion driving him towards a sharp curve to find herd of sheep passing the way. He parked on a side for relaxation and asked all to have a long breath as it been our last breath. Fresh air pumped into my lungs. *I remembered my schooling from D.A.V School where we used to do jogging in the ground, but truly I never inhaled so fresh air ever and that was only because of evil – Pollution. I felt so idealistic – wanting to go back and change the world, especially Delhi.*

The morning air was actually fresh and crisp, and despite the promise of warm sun's rays later, there was quite a cold nip in the early morning air. We jumped up and down, did sit-ups, hike on toes and did many other exercises. Sood Sir knew how great it felt to hear everyone laughing and shouting his own name. He knew how great it felt to wander freely in the mountains. Yes, if truth be told he knew how great it felt to see sun's rays appearing magically on one of the top. He reeled with the pride, knowing the excitement was all for his candidates.

'LISTEN!' He roared with the hard clap while stepping back slowly towards the camp.

'Maybe all of you know; together the Himalayan mountain system is the planet's highest, and home to the world's highest peaks, the Eight-thousanders, which include Mount Everest and K2 and geographically, it is divided into lower, middle and greater Himalayas.'

'The place where you are jogging is middle Himalayas. You are here in Uttarkashi, a town in Uttarakhand on the banks of River Bhagirathi which you very well know by name – River Ganga. Uttarkashi is a home to a number of ashrams and temples and also the Nehru Institute of Mountaineering,' he continued consistently.

'Many Himalayan peaks are sacred in Hinduism, Buddhism and Sikhism, one of which is Gangotri, from where sacred Ganges is coming out and the river which your are facing just opposite to your camp area is one of its tributary – *Asi Ganga*. The main thing you will ever notice about Himalayas is that we can never trust it. It is as dangerous, as beautiful you are finding it, particularly in terms of climate which varies from time to time. So, all of you must take care of it, mostly girls – no fashion here please. Okay.'

A kind of laughter appeared on our faces, when Mr Sood ended his small knowledgeable session about Himalayas in such a handsome way. I noticed little shyness on Anjali's face.

Unquestionably, how can my time passed without glancing her, though truthfully speaking, I tried to avoid my eyes from her while we were doing hip movement exercise.

'Hey let's all have one photograph here.' I focused all with the bridge hanging behind them.

'Hey you are standing with such a beautiful girl, buddy. Smile dear.' I said, looking past Anjali's shoulders to the guy she'd been standing with – Vivek Kaushik, a friend of Sandeep. I knew he was very sad because of his girlfriend had started dating his neighbour. For a moment, I felt the entire world was infected by the same bug of despair. The whole thought of dating – of trying to connect, trusting another person again – gave such a strong reaction that I felt a shiver go all the way down my spine. I hesitated to click but a beautiful smile saved me. She was just in the eyes of my camera, sweet and appealing. Her inner grace began to radiate outwards as I focused the zoom on her and I was damn sure that all will kill me when they will found themselves omitted from the photo and an angel on the limelight. I stood still, staring her and clicked with an effective pause. My heart got filled with the emotion. I know that not all prayers are answered but I prayed, I prayed for Anjali. Yes I understood that I was in love with her.

What if again I find my prayer unanswerable as earlier one? The thought swirled around my mind as fear but Anjali's presence, walking by my side calmed me down. I felt something there in between both of us as such our hearts were talking to each other. Well, I hoped I am also worth for her. We were just few steps away from the camp when we both stopped to climb one rock. Anjali, unsure of climbing the rock, tried to do but her foot slipped. I took a deep breath and offered her my hand. We gazed at each other for a long moment. She could almost feel that I wanted to feel her and she took a small step forward, so she could accept my offer.

This was the moment – were either of us going to make an effort to become friends? Or were we going to silently acknowledge that we had nothing in common and let it go at that? Certainly, there was something that was pulling us towards each other.

Faraway places, two people were in contact now. How? Through their hearts and souls, not through the spoken words. I had never had it with Shubhi. But I had it with Anjali, and knew – suddenly, with every nerve in my body – that she was with me now.

'Hope you have forgiven me,' she said while offering me her hand.

'Oh! Yes, without doubt'. I answered with an elastic pull.

'Thanks,' reply came with an engaging smile on her face. She appeared to be breathing silent sigh that she climbed the rock safely and I forgave her for the mistake for which in fact I didn't mind.

'You're welcome,' I responded enthusiastically.

Then, nodding, she moved towards her tent. While waiting for the girls inside tent to open the zip, she heard me murmuring a sweet love song while I passed her. She took a deep breath, amazed by the growing realisation: perhaps she was feeling the same for me that I was feeling for her. Perhaps, like all girls she was also thinking of her own world – of the simple small house, of the life full of love. Perhaps, she thought of two children and a pet dog with a belt in his neck. Perhaps she thought of a guy, somehow connected to all of it – to all of the luminous and ordinary things that had come to matter most to her. And perhaps she thought of me, the only thing I was very much interested to know.

I still don't know what I was doing there. That afternoon, I lay loosened at the side of *Asi Ganga*, feeling the warm rays of sun and watching small mother bird feeding water to her child from her own beak.

Where half of mind was waiting for the development of four groups, eight people in each, and accepting me and Anjali in same group, another half was drowning me in misery. Normally, I never let myself get this down, but today I couldn't help. It seemed like I was falling in my own thoughts, almost deceased. I was miles and miles away from my home and with no real hope of ever finding love. Sure, I had my own fantasies, but then I had to face the facts – there was no way I would ever see Shubhi again . . . at least in near future and of course at *Base Camp,* I was not sure about Anjali's feeling.

'Hey Dhruv.' I looked up to see Sandeep standing behind, smiling.

I tried to smile back. 'Hi,' I mumbled.

Sandeep dropped down at my side. 'Whole morning you were looking fresh, happy, and enjoying everything. Even at breakfast your jokes made everyone smiling. But now you're not looking so good. What happen?'

Great. Just what I needed – someone to reinforce my negative feelings. 'This is what I am. I don't like others to feel my pain.' I thought.

'Thanks a lot,' I said sarcastically.

He laughed and shook his head. 'That's not what I meant buddy. You just seem pretty down.'

I sighed and sat up straight. 'First day of trip wasn't a party for me either.'

His dark eyes glittered with amusement. 'What happened to the guy who loves adventure?'

I let out a heavy sigh. 'Listen, I am not in a good mood,' I warned him. 'So if you want to tease me, now is not the time to do it.'

Sandeep stood. 'Okay, I will give you your space. But did you think, I could help you feel close to her?'

'Ugh.' I sighed, feeling bad for having snapped at him. He understood. But how would Sandeep know that? As depressed as I was, I couldn't help smiling at his offer.

I glanced up – Sandeep was walking out of my view. 'Hey Sandeep,' I called after him.

He stopped in place and turned around. 'Yes?'

'How do you came to know?' I said.

'We both had spent so much time together,' he said.

'Oh! Ya, thanks.'

He shrugged. 'That's what friends are for. And don't forget, in half an hour, all have to assemble for group division.' Then he turned around again and headed towards tent.

I lay back down; feeling more relaxed than I had in hours. At least I had one real friend in Uttarkashi who understands me, who knows me, who cares for me. My mind was silent, remembering the words of Sandeep – regarding to be closer to Anjali. Yes, this is what I wanted. This is what my heart was waiting. I wanted to be closer to her, I wanted to know her, to feel her, and honestly I wanted to be with her. And this was not possible without being in the same group.

'Life really felt miserable without LOVE. In fact, we human are hungry for it. We turned to the side wherever we found love as such it is the only medicine for loneliness and despair. But I could never understand how many times love can solve out the problem of despair. First breakup – then love, second breakup – another love and so on. Is there any limit for the love or today it's just remaining as a topic for some talented directors to earn few lakhs or crores?' Thought appeared firmly in my mind.

But I was wrong. Love is there, all around us, only we need to search it.

In spite of the positive energy that I felt in the light of River Ganges at Haridwar, I also realised that power goes into our love according to the feeling and trust behind it. I felt the same in small dotty eyes of baby bird when mother bird had started teaching her how to fly. And I realised the power of trust that binds me with my family and friends, I realised the power that was creating my love with this new place, I realised the power of trust that was giving me assurance of Anjali to be on my side.

For many times, I gave many lectures to my friends and others regarding love and life, but it was first time after break up with Shubhi, I comprehended that the two – positive energy of love and power of trust were somewhere missing in my own soul. I lived my life with my own fear; my own beliefs and those inner negative assumptions ruled and governed my life. The belief had no power in and of itself. Its power arises from the fact that we must accept it mentally. Like a sailor had no fear of seasickness, a lover should not have despair sickness but every time my stupid possessiveness increased the distance between me and Shubhi and I lost her.

So, to override my thoughts I did the same. I formulated a very simple and direct prayer.

I think, speak, and act lovingly, quietly, and peacefully. I now radiate love, peace, and tolerance to all those who criticised me and gossiped about me. I anchor my thought on peace, harmony, and goodwill to all.

Whenever I am about to react negatively, I say firmly to myself – 'I think, speak, and act from the standpoint of the principle of harmony, health, and peace within myself. Fait will lead, rule and govern me in all my ways.'

We used to say the same in the school during early Morning Prayer but very honestly, this was the first time I actually understood what it meant for and finally, with the positive energy that River Ganges showered on me along with the power of trust bestowed to me by a baby bird, I moved towards my new family.

I was hovering at the edge of the camp, watching the people introducing themselves more clearly in their new group with few pats on the back.

Come on, Anjali, I said silently to myself. *I'm waiting for you! I'm here!*

I pressed my right hand lightly against my heart – my heartbeat was hammering away. Had I ever been this excited? Well, there had been my birthday, when I'd closed my eyes to find a new laptop waiting for me. But what was a Compaq Intel core 2 duo processor compared to the knowledge that my long – distance love wasn't long distance after all?

It was Anjali heading towards me. It was Sandeep, Vivek, Nitin, Manish, Partho and another girl – Shilpa, seven other members of Group A, with one Instructor Mr Sood. Four groups were finally formed with four different instructors.

"Hi,' I turned my eyes away from all and turned to Anjali. But my tempo rose a little, when Vivek interrupted in between. 'Uh, I was thinking it might be a good idea, let's all have a look on our ten days schedule. All details have been displayed there on the notice board.' He said.

'Schedule!' I exclaimed. 'Let's leave that thing as a surprise buddy and face the facts and deals. Just chill, enjoy and welcome everything to come as something natural and unknown.' Words came out promptly from my lips as I don't know what this guy's problem was, and at that moment I didn't care. I just wanted to run up and hug Anjali. I stepped back from Sandeep so that I could see her clearly.

Each group started to have their meeting in small circles and we did the same when our instructor instructed.

'So, welcome all of you again to the camp.'

'Thank You Sir.' All said together.

'So, before giving you any instructions or any idea about your camp, can we have a small introduction? Yeah, may be all of you know each other, but I also have a right to know about my team.' Mr Sood continued.

Smile appeared on all faces. He was really a gentleman and his body language was seriously attracting all. So likewise, introduction session repeated again but this was really much better than the earlier.

'Okay that's perfect. You all seemed to be really well and very much excited,' Sood Sir exclaimed when Nitin – a slim, weatish and also younger one among all of us ended the introduction.

'Yes Sir.' Every voice was loud and energetic.

'Good. So first of all, as all of you know that you are here for ten long days, therefore, it's my duty to give you an idea for the same.

Over seven centuries ago, there was a poet called - Sa'di. He wrote very beautiful lines:

The children of Adam are limbs of one body
Having been created of one essence.
When the calamity of time afflicts one limb
The other limbs cannot remain at rest.
If you have no sympathy for the troubles of others
You are not worthy to be called by the name of "man."

Meaning, here in this camp if u want to sustain, you should not forget that like you, all have same feelings. Not only, you all have to be together, but, here, you all need to be together. This is the place where you will actually know what you are, what you can do and what you actually deserve. You shouldn't only behave like a team, but you have to LIVE your every minute as a team.' He said continuously. It seemed that some powerful waves passed away from our body.

'You will definitely enjoy here but only you must be positive. You must be ready mentally for everything as here you will feel that mental power is more important than the physical. For the first five days, we all remain here at base camp only and experience many adventurous activities, and rest five days we will trek to *Darwa Top*, 13,500 ft. above sea level, for which you actually came here.'

'And I promise that you will not only enjoy this trip but these ten days will become the most memorable days of your life.'

'You just need to follow three simple things:

- As you would want people to think about you, think about them in the same manner.

- As you would want people to feel about you, feel about them in the same manner.
- As you would want people to act toward you, act toward them in the same manner.'

'Okay.'

'Yes Sir.'

He was right. Those ten days were really the most memorable days of my life.

'Sir, I think you should be a speaker or motivational programmer,' Shilpa said surprisingly while loosening her blonde hairs that I remembered very well.

'Yeah, she is right.' Manish, who seemed not to be less than any playboy, supported with such an idiotic smile, that I thought to smash down his teeth that time only but thanks to the three points of Mr Sood that helps me perfectly to overrule my negativity.

'Thanks for that. But I am not a speaker. I am only Sandeep Sood and that's only what I always wanted to be.' Sood Sir said very calmly.

'That's really nice of you Sir. Sir, May I please know what the height of this base camp is?' Partho, the smart, little fatty guy, wearing black goggles, asked curiously. He seemed to be very silent and polite but his branded clothes and cap was exposing his cool stud form.

'It's about 4,300 ft.' The frequent reply came from the opposite side.

Although sunlight was low now, but it seemed so natural, that sitting there in the sunshine, just like a family, I thought, glancing briefly round at the other faces. And likewise while concentrating on our lunch, under the shade of the sun that was doing its function very well and with the feel of cold air which was somehow bantering us, we engrossed in some conversation regarding "tolerance for adversity and uncertainty" – something we knew and cared about. We also acknowledged more interesting things about Himalayas, Its flora and fauna, about our program, our trekking route and about each other.

Right from the point, I wanted to build up an environment of faith, trust and respect among all and it felt good to feel that it didn't take much time to get fixed in the group. All my team members were really good, well-mannered and very friendly. All my plans for this break, involving free time, friends, photo shoots and peace seemed to be almost achieved and it was also more cleared that first five days at base camp would be devoted to different kind of activities, whatever that meant. It was from sixth day onwards that the trekking experience would begin. As per Mr Sood, during the complete program, we will learn what we are made of. We will learn the importance of team work. We will learn to trust our life to our partners when necessary. And we will emerge as a better human.

We looked down the instruction sheet; copies had just been distributed to all. Sandeep read one point loudly, may be that aggravated him most: *All will be segregated by sex for sleeping purpose, though they will work with their team in all other activities.*

But everything was really excited, not less than any fun. I was very happy, perhaps because I had made new friends, or perhaps because I was not alone, or perhaps because Anjali was looking more beautiful – even more beautiful than the photograph that I'd taken, or perhaps because, we were in same group or perhaps because she was sitting just next to me and I could feel the fragrance of her body very clearly.

I felt amazingly happy. While all were reading their sheets, my eyes were fix on her. She was also looking into the sheet. I could have stayed there forever continuously observing her, yet some interesting games activities, important session on Rucksack packing, daily routine of filling tanks, and the frozenness of the evening that had come down, making us shivering involuntarily became barrier in between and we departed.

Someone said right: *Time never remains the same*.

It was uncanny, I felt the way I had in hell, when I'd been pissing behind one tree, looked across, and saw Anjali – where she shouldn't have been, where the chances were one in million for us to meet. Needless to say, I was not enchanted, even though I couldn't help noticing her. She was wandering with Shweta and their feet were approaching where I was trying to hide. So, I just came out suddenly in order to replace the fact of my doing by the joke of frightening them. Both of them got afraid. I could feel them breathing heavily.

I am stupid. Right? I thought so, but I guess it made me sort of relief also as they didn't saw what I was actually doing.

'Are you always crazy like this?' I was in deep thought when Shweta asked me rigidly.

'Only when I try to make good impression on someone.' I said while staring at Anjali, but there seemed to be some strange expression on her face as such she was not happy welcoming me, as such I was irritating her.

It was only six. Cloud raced across the moon; the light passed over. Darkness, light, darkness, light . . . the area was illuminated by the moon, then dark again. Shweta's smiling and little bit of teasing departure made me sure that she had a little idea of my feelings. But what was this, Anjali was also leaving.

'Hey, you are not nervous, are you?' I said

'Why could I possibly be nervous?'

'I know, this is your first day here and maybe you are thinking that I am trying to talk to you again and again, but listen, I am not such a bad guy. Don't go by me. I am not dangerous.' Though she was standing little sideways to me, but I could notice something problematic on her face. She turned.

'What do you want?' a little harsh voice asked me slowly.

'A small walk with a beautiful girl,' I said firmly.

She said nothing for some time and started staring at me.

'Hey what happened? Looks like you ran into something.' I asked curiously.

'Nothing. It's just – well, you just don't look like the type who goes around girls, that's all.' Words shattered me suddenly.

That really got me. I mean, what did she know about me, anyway? Just because she happened to be lovable beautiful, didn't give her the right to go around judging people like this. All my thoughts till the time, regarding her feelings, seemed to burn away in fire. She was taking me as someone loafer. I hoped she wasn't serious; she was only joking, but for some reasons I felt like crying. However, I wasn't about to let her know how I was feeling. I felt down. My heart seemed to be burst as such I saw any nightmare.

'Actually, I won the first prize for running after girls.' I tossed back coolly in the hope that she would reply something positive. There were probably many boys who had crushes on her and she was probably counting me as one more like them. Maybe she was thinking that I was just trying to play with her.

I knew by that time there is nothing special in me for which any girl will love me. Not that I'm smart or anything. I'm very average looking. My hairs are short, my eyes are dark black. I am just 5.5, slim with no body built. I think my nose is big, but maybe it's my only imagination since no one ever said anything about it.

I fixed my gaze on her. 'What was taking so long?' I willed her to hurry up. Thank God! Right then, though, I could have felt lonelier if she had not agreed to spend some time with me. She just moved few steps with me and we sat down to have some more conversation. Her behaviour was confusing me. It seemed that she wanted to ask me something. I was not sure either she wanted to be with me or not. Really, to understand girls is not less than the task to jump into any well. All through that time she continued to plague me. I came to know the fact that she was counting me among the guys who liked to play with girl's sentiments.

'It's better to have some distance with her' I thought. It was strictly my imagination which made it seem as if there was something going on between us, and there definitely was not. During my complete program, I decided to play the part of a good human, good friend and good team member only. Her line '*the type who goes around the girls*' had bouncing affect on my mind.

'And also tell me one thing. What makes you so sure that I'm interested in whether or not you think I'm beautiful? If you are thinking that I apologize you for baptising you as an idiot, it doesn't mean that you will say that I want to do friendship with you or I am behind you.'

'What?' I shouted. Now, I understood why all this happened. So, this was the reason why she was behaving like that.

'But I have said nothing like this,' I said in defense.

'You just keep quiet,' she said. It seemed like everyone knew what was going on between me and her. I could see number of faces encircling both of us. The matter was seriously going out of my hand, and it's seriously needed to do something.

'You just keep quiet Miss Anjali, whatever your full name is. I haven't said anything like this to anyone. Whoever told you these words just make him or her stand in front of me now, truly whatever punishment all will give, I will accept heartedly. Just make the person stand here right now.' I said last words very loudly.

'Shweta,' she leaked out very toughly. I could see that she got little frightened too.

Everyone was confused. Every eye was fixed at Shweta. Her head was down. No one said anything for some time.

'I was just kidding,' a simple reply came from her mouth. Anjali got shattered by the reply. I am sure she felt very much embarrassed.

'Miss Anjali. Firstly please confirm before taking any decision and never try to judge anyone in future like this.' I just said in anger. I was very sad, not only because what Anjali thought for me, but also because it provided a matter of gossip to all. The most incredible part was that she started crying and just ran away to the tent. I was so stunned that I couldn't move. But I sighed relax when Sandeep consoled me down.

'My first day would be so worst, I never thought of.' I was very angry. 'It's really better to be away even from the reflection of her,' thought appeared in my mind the whole evening. Dinner seemed to be tasteless. Somewhere I could sense that the topic of me and Anjali was still fresh in every mind. I tried to look for Anjali. Her face was dull, as such she had cried for many hours. I had never thought that this could happen anyhow. All positive energy and power of trust appeared to be buried deep inside the small chambers of my heart. I felt a few eyes on me even after I turned my back. It sounds so dumb. 'Seriously, it's better to be away from her' thought rose again in my mind when I noticed with irritation that Shweta was gossiping with her friends so coolly as such she had done nothing. I wanted to shout at her, but....

'I don't know how anyone could say anything about anyone,' I said adamantly. 'What's her problem?' 'Fuck' I groaned, more from pain – pain of despair before formation of pair. My heart was slamming against my rib cage. But one hand was still there.

'You OK?' Sandeep asked. 'Ya. I am alright.' He was still consoling me. Once again he'd succeeded in making me feel like relaxed. I took a deep breath. It was really nice to be with him there.

Later, the very same day, there was a video show on First Indian lady on Everest. It was the time of get-together; the camp was transformed into a magical arena under the stars, with some fireflies glowing around and a projector beaming on a small screen. It seemed as such we were sitting in an open air theatre. Groups had already taken their places. Freezing air made all wore everything from warm inners to woolen caps and gloves. The night was very romantic. I was with the girl I loved, in the place where we met and where we depart. But where all were excited, gossiping, waiting for the video to be started, we two were in mute mode, little embarrassed, somehow little frustrated and angry.

'What is wrong with you two, please sort out?' Sandeep said softly.

'I am sorry,' Anjali said while making a crying face.

'No miss, I am sorry,' I replied solidly in a taunting manner. Actually I was a fool, I realised later. I shouldn't try to be oversmart that time.

'Okay, it means you really don't like her, do you?' Sandeep scrutinised me. His question shocked Anjali but she said nothing.

'No, I don't like her. I hate her!' Words appeared on my lips both very suddenly and toughly.

'Rinni says that when a person says that he/she hates someone it's really a kind of backward love,' said Sandeep with a well-founded laugh.

Rinni is Sandeep's friend. She wears her dark black hair in a ponytail and how could I forget to mention about her dimples whichs make her look like as she was kicked in the face by a donkey, though Sandeep thinks they are adorable. I think he has a crush on her.

'You could turn her upside down I will still said the same. And suppose if I say yes I like her, then it will mean that I am the type who goes around the girls. Right.' Sandeep could sense love in my tone. I could tell she also suspected that I was saying the truth, that I like her, but she just couldn't bring herself out and ask. Maybe she wanted to avoid the topic.

'And Anjali you, do you want to say anything or just want to sit stupidly like this only.'

'I don't want to say anything,' she said in little sobbing voice. She probably wouldn't want to talk about it anyway.

'Listen very carefully. Whatever had happened, forget it. The two of you both are too stubborn to admit that you could probably like each other if you ever gave it a try and somebody definitely has to start first.' Sandeep declared very calmly as such he was trying to make us one.

Anjali made a loud, strangled noise. 'Will you guys please let up? What is this – *you like each other* or *gave a try*. I am only sad for what I did. There was nothing like that. If you guys think that I am in love, then please, never think of this.'

'I can only say I am sorry and request all of you to behave like a good team member.' She ended and left the place.

Everything seemed to be shattered again. It was like an old saying '*History repeats itself*'. I was almost traumatised as such something had been busted somewhere inside me.

From the day I kept my foot out of college, I only realised one thing that girls are actually smarter than boys and it's really difficult to understand them. They are not less than any poison, though there is one difference that poison kills you promptly, but girls, oh God, they kill you slowly.

The truth wasn't so terrible when I compared it to the time I spent with Shubhi, but it was a problem nevertheless as I didn't want to face the same problem again. I knew Anjali had not done right that she blamed me for the mistake I hadn't done, but she was not someone I could easily hate, even if I tried, which believe me, I had.

Actually I wouldn't have minded Anjali as only team member, but whenever the subject of love came up, I got sick. Whenever I saw her, my eyeballs came out. Whenever I heard her voice, my heartbeats started thrashing. I guess nothing would really change since I left Delhi. It still worried me because of love, though it was not Shubhi now, I accepted. It was funny also as I never thought that I could be in love again even after six months trauma. But I knew the fact that to slay the pain of one person departure, another one need to arrive. What kind of relationship do I and Anjali have? I wondered. It was still so new and strange that I had a hard time believing the whole episode on the camp wasn't something my feverish brain cooked up.

No one knew exactly that I was dying for her. I tried to talk Sandeep about it again, but it was when the voice of some lady pulled me strongly.

'If God save me from such a disaster, it means there is something left that still I have to do.' She said positively after escaping safely from snow ice Avalanche in 1984. Perhaps, it was just few kms before the summit, when she faced such a

tragedy. All mountaineers were badly shaken and refused to go further, but she accepted the challenge and raised the flag on top. The video was actually regarding emerging women power and her journey to reach the summit of Everest. The video reveals the limit of confidence, positive energy and spirit, one could have. The difficulties she encountered during the long and arduous journey to Everest has been an experience of lifetime, which will help all of us to face the future challenges with new confidence and strength.

Truly, the video was very motivating and filled all of us with new courage. It gave birth to new enthusiasm in all our heart. All wanted to start the trek as soon as possible. New wave seemed to be generated in me also. If positively admit, a new confidence became native in my soul. I aroused again from all my pain and confusion. My trust rose again slowly, and as I stepped along in my sleeping bag, I thought about what Anjali had said about me. She was right, I realised, though I didn't say the words to Shweta, but I was the only one who was taking all interactions as love. I got embarrassed when I thought about the things I'd said to her. I didn't really excite her all that much, there was no surprise now. But I liked it that way. 'Our relationship will be safe like this only' I thought. 'As I want to spend some time with her, it will only be possible, as being a good team member. In any case, she never said that she loves me. It was me only who gave birth to such thoughts, then why to worry.'

I had no control over what has just happened. What happened next will be determined by how I react. I bother. I harshly scold her for blaming me for the mistake I have not done. She breaks down in tears. A short verbal battle then follows. As it continues, it seems to get worse and worse.

I looked forward to talk to her, but I found a small wedge in between.

And why all this happened? Just because of my reaction that evening. And who caused it? – Shweta, Anjali or me. Yes, it was me. I had no control over whatever I said. How I reacted in those 20 seconds is what caused my evening bad.

Here is what could have been done and should have happened. She blamed, I shouted, she started crying and I gently says, "It's OK dear, you just need to be clearer next time before blaming anyone."

Powerful lively video taught me that something good might come out from our sufferings. It's really foolish to continue to suffer. She gave me a confidence to fill my life with love, to fulfill my desires. She gave me a spirit to live every minute as mine. She gave me a power to admit my love. Yes, I have to admit I was well past that feeling. I'd been sure of our team relationship. But now I didn't know what would happen between us. Though I was little scared, but the two days had already taught me three big lessons of life – to be positive, confident and faithful. I felt a great sense of peace and satisfaction.

And as I finally decided 'I will admit my love - I will definitely propose her,' it seemed that some burden had been flown away from my heart and after having done so, my mind got quiet, relax, let go and got into a drowsy, sleepy state that reduces my mental efforts to a minimum. Even, if I was not happy, I was not even sad. I was very well comforted in my warm sleeping bag waiting for the best time, the time when I could expose my feelings directly to her.

Mountaineering, Rappelling and Flying Fox – words itself seemed to be very excited and dangerous, and I swear they were really very excited, though not so dangerous as most of the girls feel. Climbing them might result to something hazardous but stuff was actually good regarding safety. It was Rappelling time – around 125 feet I could see two ropes hanging down from the top. On our movement up to the site, Anjali had said as little as possible to me. She hadn't commented one way or the other on the fact that we were team members. Even I didn't give any indication that I found her cute, or even remotely interesting. Mostly I did what I had to do and kept my mouth shut. Might be she felt that I was also feeling sorry for the whole drama took place yesterday. My heart was still pounding, and I felt as if I was missing her a lot. I was both devastated and exhilarated – a dangerous combination. But I would manage to find my own way. And I would continue to find the best time, no matter what happened between her and me.

And in the meantime, all groups were ready for rappelling with their leaders and instructions for the same have been given to us by Sood Sir:

'So, the very type of mountaineering you are ready to do is called Rappelling or Abseiling. In this you have to rope down from here very safely and please don't look behind while you rope down. Just stretch yourself as much as you can and step down slowly. Okay.'

'Yes Sir.' Group A was ready with all high spirits.

'Good. So before beginning let me confirm; all of you must hear the story of a tortoise and rabbit in the childhood.'

'Yes Sir.'

'Anyone can please tell me what the Moral of the story was?'

'Sir.' Vivek raised the hand very confidently.

'Yes.'

'Moral: Slow and Steady wins the race.'

'That's good. But can anyone tell me what happens after the rabbit realised that he had lost the race.' Sood sir asked calmly but every face was blank. 'Okay, no problem. I will tell. So, all you know till the tortoise overtook the rabbit and soon finished the race, emerging as winner.' He continued while all heads nodded simultaneously.

'The rabbit was disappointed at losing the race and then, he did "think there must be some better way". He realised that he had lost the race only because he had been overconfident, careless and lazy. If he had not taken things for granted, there's no way that tortoise could have beaten him. So he challenged the tortoise to another race. The tortoise agreed. This time, the rabbit went all out and ran without stopping from start to finish. He won by several miles.'

'Moral: Fast and consistent will always beat the slow and steady. It's good to be slow and steady; but it's better to be fast and consistent, also!'

We all got little surprised and might be he judged that surprise on our face. But he said nothing and continued further.

'The story is still not complete my friends. The tortoise did some thinking this time, and realised that there's no way he can beat the rabbit in a race the way it was currently formatted. He thought for a while, and then challenged the rabbit to another race, but on a slightly different route. The rabbit agreed. They started off. In keeping with his self-made commitment to be consistently fast, the rabbit took off and ran at top speed until he came to a river. The finishing line was a couple of kilometres on the other side of the river. The rabbit sat there wondering what to do. In the meantime tortoise kept along, got into the river, swam to the opposite bank, continued walking and finished the race.'

'Moral: First identify your competency and your strength and then follow your path.'

'And last more improvement. The rabbit and the tortoise, by this time, had become good friends and they did some thinking together. Both realised that they can race for mutual advantage. So they decided to run the race again, but this time, to run as a team. They started off, and this time the rabbit carried the tortoise till the river bank. Then, the tortoise took over and swam across with the rabbit on his back. On the opposite bank, the rabbit again carried the tortoise and they reached the finishing line together. They both felt a great sense of happiness, satisfaction and success.'

'Now, Moral: It is good to be individually motivated and to have strong capabilities: but unless you are able to work in a team and harness each other's capabilities, you will always perform below par because there will always be situations at which you'll do poorly and someone else does well. Note that neither the rabbit nor the tortoise gave up after failure. Both succeeded and enjoyed the pleasure of winning together.'

'So, now all of you have to rope down from here, two parallely to each other. It's up to you either you want to rope down speedily as rabbit did or you want to clear your path and move like tortoise or you want to chose any other way. But be clear that you must reach your goal very safely.'

'Everything cleared.' Sood Sir concluded calmly.

'Yes Sir.' Confident voices again rose in the mountains.

The bad news was that I was the first to rope down; the good news was being parallely with a partner who apparently had no intention of carrying on the simplest of conversations.

Subsequently, all members of Group A were ready once again for the battle field, ready to get organised for their next job: cheering for me and Anjali. All except Ms Poonam, of course, who had already rope down to a site deep in hills to show us a demo and positively to support the participants from there.

'I have a bad feeling about this.' Anjali murmured to Shilpa as she holds the rope in her hands, tucked with Ceraviner. She was standing so close to me, I could smell mint on her breath.

Time runs. Woo-Woo. Stepping behind slowly to the edge of the hill was seriously exciting, though my heartbeats were throbbing heavily.

Fuck! The word came out of my mouth abruptly as I sllpped off at edge and hanged up in the air. Thank God balance maintained. But I could sense fear in the eyes of Anjali who was as well hanged by my side. Though the situation was somewhere serious but thought of two bodies hanging together, especially me and Anjali, made me slightly laugh too. But I hold myself again and continue my journey slowly. It was when I crossed almost half of my path, the story of rabbit and tortoise stroked in my head. I raised my neck to see Anjali. She was just moving like the tortoise, slow and steady. I think she was not feeling comfortable. 'I must help her' thought came in my mind.

To tell you the truth, I am not a big rule follower. So, frankly I didn't care. I forgot about an important instruction that I should not try to climb back. So, I did the same but I am not feeling shame to admit that my body strength didn't support me well and I left with one option waiting for her. I could hear the voices 'Come on Dhruv… Move… Come on… You can do it'. Hey I knew that I can rope down but how could I explain you the reason while suspending there. Idiots or maybe I was a superior Idiot who was waiting for the girl in such a situation.

Finally, she joined. I turned to her and we stared at each other for a while. She was quiet for few minutes. Her hands were trembling, and she was very slow. She even gave me a dark look.

'How I got here – that's what you wanted to know,' I said slowly. 'Actually I was walking to McDonalds down there to have a burger and Pepsi, and then I saw you coming behind. So, I stopped in the hope that you will like to join me. After all, you are also feeling tired.' I said stupidly.

I couldn't help it – she laughed. Yes, she giggled. Thank God.

'Hey miss, I am so sorry for yesterday.' I continued with a gap in the hope that she will react positively.

'Don't be,' Anjali said. 'It was not your mistake.' She said with a smile. We forgot that were stuck somewhere seriously.

'Move you both. Move.' Voice banged in my ears from the top. It was Sood sir, pulling my rope heavily. 'Hey Dhruv, move. There are …….. also waiting …………. turn.' Some words were unapproachable because of distance but I understood that we have to move.

'If you like we can choose the fourth part of the rabbit-tortoise's story,' I said while offering her my hand. But she hesitated this time. I told her that they were the words 'as a friend', which made her feel little comfortable and she held my hand smoothly.

Hey Sandeep Sir, thanks, thanks for that story. We leaned our back parallely and folded our hands into each other's. We were almost arrested.

We were moving as safely as we could but she again slipped off. I wrapped my arms around her as a support. It was then when I heard lots of whistles. We guys – really fool, I understood first time.

After a beat of silence, Anjali said. 'Thanks.'

'No need miss.'

So, the journey started again and it was when I stepped my feet speedily, 'Hey Dhruv, are you mad, move slowly, please,' she said fearfully.

I controlled my steps and tried to move slowly.

'You know. Everyone is mad on this planet. Some for money, some for love, some for food, some for fame and some for their stupid dreams. Everyone is MAD but only the degree of madness for all is different.' I said.

I think she was in a hurry to ask something but all of a sudden, Ms Poonam holds us from behind until we set our foot positively. So, we reached and sat down on the rock. The sun was high in the sky and quite bright.

'That's why you introduced yourself as MAD.'

'Yes.' I assured.

'And Dhruv is MAD for?' her sudden question shot me for a while. I got speechless. But I should also reply her. I was puzzled. So, I just laugh in order to avoid the conversation what I found better that time. I couldn't tell her about the perplexity, I was dumped in, regarding Shubhi and her.

Right! So I laughed more.

'What happen?'

'Nothing.'

'I think you are a philosopher?' Anjali continued.

'No.' I smiled and just moved from there to have some water from the stream flowing nearby. Hope she hadn't sensed any tension on my face.

'Where are you going?'

'Don't you want a burger and Pepsi?'

She smiled again. I could feel that she was no more angry but I knew that this was not the time for which I was waiting impatiently; therefore, I cupped my hands in order to kill my thirst. Thank God! I said.

Oh No! In all excitement, I forgot to tell you about Rappelling. Hahahahahaha.

Rappelling – Ya, it was really a great experience. You almost feel like you are suspending in between life and death. Watching downwards is like you are gone. It seems that all senses stopped working for a while. What? What do you ask? Why this is not happened with me? Hey buddy, all this happened, that's why I am telling you, right! But actually what happened is that something inside me helped me to overrule such fears and that was the power to love. And it was that which make me strong, strong enough to support Anjali. I don't know how others felt when they rope down from the same after me. I don't know what others were saying about me and Anjali. What I know that I really felt a great sense of satisfaction, peace and happiness. Yes, I actually enjoyed my turn.

All three, Mountaineering, Rappelling and Flying Fox were as much exciting as adventurous they were. It takes almost five-to-six hours for whole task to be completed by all. Anshuman and Nishit, the two great rascals, rappelled twice cheatingly.

Everyone was excited and happy after experiencing such a wonderful and adventurous fixture.

While jogging back up to the top of the hill so that we could step back to base camp, '*Good Job*' many told me. Among them some were actually appreciate me for my task and some maybe to tease me, but I didn't care. I was happy. I was happy because of someone whom I stared at whole day, sometimes from behind the bushes, sometimes while we were engaged in different activities, sometimes while moving through various paths and sometimes, just by closing my eyes.

Everything seemed to be awesome, like some sort of a bridge was slowly taking shape in between me and Anjali. I felt like I was back in my life, before any of this other stuff happened.

My heart was a drumbeat. This was the real deal. I love her. But there went my heart again to the question 'And Dhruv is MAD for?' That kiss under the tree had lasted a fully ten minutes. I can never forget her. Yes I can never. This bloody HEART, *Ugh!*

What am I going to tell Shubhi that I am in love with someone else? What am I going to tell her if by chance we met ever again? She was right that some other girl will replace her easily. Are we guys actually like this? No, Yes, No, I don't know actually is it a case only with guys or every human. Maybe in her life too, somebody had already taken my place also. Do Actually?

The same question repeated itself in my head again and again. Now that I liked another girl, the utter absurdity of my words '*No one can take your place*' had been able to sink in. How could I have let this go so far?

And also something more serious that was playing with me.

What am I going to tell Anjali that she is not the first girl of my life? What am I going to tell her that there is someone else who still has some place in my heart? Are we guys actually like this? No, Yes, No, I don't know actually is it a case only with guys or every human. Maybe in her life too, I will not be the first guy. Do Actually?

I was totally perplexed. The whole above reactions seemed to me like a quarrel going on among me, my heart, my mind and my soul. My life was not less than any mess. My heart was tore into pieces, like playing some song –

My heart tore into thousands of pieces;
Some fell here some fell there.....

It only wants to be with someone special. It wants to cry. My mind, what to say – It was ordering me to be away from all emotional drama. And my soul, it was making me realize about the importance of love, the promises I made with myself, my family and my friends – not to be sad. It was asking me to tell Anjali about Shubhi. Within a few seconds, I felt almost murdered, seemed like my senses has lost its power to think, to decide my good.

'Are you mooning over someone – or just enjoying the moon?'

Startled, I looked up to find Anjali walking toward me. 'Anjali! Hi!' Was my voice unnaturally bright? Was it obvious that I was trying to hide my guilt for involving her in my life as someone special?

'Nothing,' I declared.

All right, now she was making me mad. Sure, this wasn't the shining moment in my life as a worthwhile human being. We were sitting quiet like Idiots.

'Hey, can you please tell me how am I?' My words shocked her actually.

'What?' her eyebrows shot up?

'Don't take me wrong. I just want to know, what you think what type of guy I am?' I said. I could sense some confusion on her face. 'I don't mean that. I mean what's my nature according to you? Mean…' I continued but suddenly she started laughing. I got confused. I was a fool in fact. But everything I was doing was for the sake of love. 'She obviously never had been in love. If she had, she'd understand what it like – what it can make you do' thought came in my mind.

She shook her head, staring at me with something strange in her eyes. 'Are you questioning to yourself or me?'

I said nothing. I was feeling a little embarrassed too. Whatever it was, attraction or love, it was just next to me. It was a kind of familiar sensation that wrapped me for a while. I took a deep breath and just kept quiet staring at the moon again until she moved back to her tent without saying anything.

Closing my eyes against the glare of the small bulb lightening in my tent, I allowed reality to come crashing down. Things between me and Anjali weren't exactly wonderful. The bridge needs some more time to be formed. I don't know what she was actually thinking about me. Was she making fun of me? Or our still unknown relationship was an utter joke. Sandeep had been right all along. I never should allow my feelings to hike so much that I myself will feel like get burdened.

I had to find a way to make Anjali realize that she had to choose me and me only. But will it be right? Should I interfere in the work of destiny? But I couldn't wait. *I think they were my testosterones or genes that were making me feel like this.* I was completely bewildered. But today I know that it was not Shubhi's memory which was puzzling me. It was my loneliness which was playing with my sentiments, which was confusing me, which was making me embarrass. It was the sadness to be alone. It was not Shubhi for whom I was MAD. I was MAD for love like every human being.

All my life, I accepted everything because I believe that "Everything happens for a good reason", but critically that time I was like drowned in fathomless sea of thoughts and there was nobody to save me. For the time being, everything I learned – to be positive, faithful, everything seemed to be like exploded.

Actually what the fact is that we humans need someone to hear us, to be with us, to kill our lonesomeness, to love us madly. And that was what I wanted. But I didn't understand the same that time and got lost into swirl of thoughts.

'Should I tell her about Shubhi?' I was confused.

In any case, how can I forget that the girls are actually smarter than boys, and it's really difficult to understand them.

So, rather than behaving like an Idiot, I just need to be patient and let leave everything as it was going on. I must challenge my luck this time. I must.

So, trying to be habitual, I thanked God again and got packed into my sleeping bag.

After all, this was do-or-die time. If my feelings were true, I was going to succeed, or I was going to be crashed and burnt. Either way the nightmare would soon be over.

Chapter 2

Crazy Instinct

From the day I kept my foot in the college I realised that all boys are actually Idiots. And my dear friends, I was right. Here is the live example in front of You - Dhruv Gupta – a big idiot in small package, a duffer about whom I always thought that today he will definitely propose me. But seriously, I don't know till now, why he didn't. Why he always seemed to be so confused, so worried?

I guess a lot of things had always worried me also. It's funny though. If you're fairly pretty and somewhat popular and don't have too much trouble in getting dates, then people think your life is practically wonderful, and you have total self-confidence. Well, that's absolutely untrue. I don't think I am all that pretty, for one thing. I'm OK, but like I said, I think maybe my mouth is too big, and I know for a fact my nose is on stubby side. Then there is a matter of dates. I can have lot, I agree but truly says, I didn't have them as like all girls I also wanted someone who will love me, not my body. Someone whose eyes will only say true, with whom my heart can conversate, and beyond doubt I don't know why I found something in this duffer. I'd only been talking to Dhruv for few days, but sometimes I felt as if we'd known each other forever.

I know sometimes we can't even look at each other without getting into an argument but how could I let him know that Girls always try to pretend like this only, that they don't love you. They never ever let you know what they actually feel. Gentleman needs to ask them directly face to face.

But after reading Part I, I am sure, either he is really a fool or he is a lover, or I think that he is a fool because he is a lover.

Thank God, he allowed me to write the second part; otherwise I am sure all would definitely laugh on his stupidity.

Hey friends, before starting my part I let you know I love Dhruv, I love him. I like him from the time when he said – "Ya! I know that, but that's their physical presence. Mentally you are alone" and slowly his attitude persisted me to love him too.

I can never forget those words. Nobody ever talk to me like this. I was seriously alone that day, missing my family, my darling younger sister – *Ananya* and my cute cat – *Kitty*. I never went away from home for so many days, especially never in the area where there was almost no network. I never spent so much time without my father.

He was the first who caught my loneliness in such a dark. That night I wept, I wept for a long time and nobody came to know. His words acutely touched my heart.

I seriously admire him; admire him for the honesty he has shown to me – the honesty with which he spends his every minute with me, with which he loves me and with which he told me everything about his past.

It was just like a few days back only. I can still recount the time. Rucksacks packed, food items issued, campsite got cleaned and groups were in queue, as per instruction. Next event was still a surprise. A small lesson on 'how to use Compass proceeded for a few minutes. And it was when Ms Poonam handed over one map to Manish, surprise came out of the box.

'Leadership Program,' Sood Sir's voice flew in our ears, 'is a life-changing experience. You are not the same person anymore, when you arrived.'

He let that sink for the moment. 'Nor are we-', he mentioned to the assembled other instructors to his left, 'the same. We rode you hard when you arrived, because when you arrived you needed to be ridden hard. But as you adjusted, so did we. Amazing, isn't it? How quickly you can grow in a very short period of time.'

All nodded in agreement.

'And the camp will end with more wonderful experiences likewise, I promise,' he continued. 'So now tell, have anyone of you heard of the Jungle camp?'

Amandeep's hand shot skyward. 'It's when you take us into the jungle and leave us there for the whole night, with some food items and tent.'

'Correct, my dear. Today, we all are going to stay in a Jungle area and that's for the whole night.' Sood Sir said.

I'm dead; sudden thought arose in my mind. 'Sir, if we get eaten by any wild animal or something.'

'Oh! Dear don't worry; there is no animal in that area. Ya, sometimes, a tiger has been found while roaming there, but nothing will happen, don't worry,' Sood Sir said very calmly.

'What?' I think everyone could sense the fear in my eyes when my voice rose to the fullest. Some creases took place on my forehead.

But suddenly Sood sir started laughing heavily. 'Just joking dear, I already said – Don't worry.'

I sighed a relief like I came back into my senses. The idea of being stuck in the jungle with any animal did not actually delight.

'So, everyone get ready, and remember you have to move with your groups; okay'

Thank God, we are in group, I thought, *or I'd have to write my undefined will before I step forward for unexplored territory.*

So, finally Sood Sir nodded at Manish to take over. Manish stepped forward. 'We think you've each gotten too comfortable with your group, so we're going to shake things up a bit. Your groups for jungle camp have been grouped geographically,'

Sood Sir told us. 'Mean two groups will go in different area and another two will be in other, okay'

All nodded. Sandeep stepped and consulted the compass again as we have to search the jungle area on our own as per the symbols on map. So, where almost everyone was excited with a smile, my senses were still a little scared.

I hoped that Dhruv could see that I'd lost that happy, relax look and try to make me feel better but that Idiot was still adjusting his Rucksack.

The next one hour was spent in a gruelling hike over rough terrain. We passed from the side of hill, which was steep and stony; a spout of gravel was dislodged, and fell rattling and bounding through the trees. Though everything was naturally beautiful, but I don't know why I was not able to saw that beautiful part and whole silence seemed to me like an eerie. Every step was like something stroked under the foot. That few metres height was really painful and thought of trekking up to Darwa Top, 13,500 ft., made my eyes little wetly too. All this while, as I say, I was still trekking, and, without taking any notice, I had drawn near to the foot of the little hill with two peaks.

And here a fresh alarm brought me to a standstill with a thumping heart, when my eyes turned instinctively in that direction and I saw a figure with great rapidity behind the trunk of pine. What it was; a tiger or man, I could in no way tell? It seemed bushy. But the terror of this new apparition brought me to a stand. I was now, it seemed, cut off upon both sides; beneath me a hard trail, before me this lurking nondescript. And immediately I began to prefer the dangers that I knew to those that I knew not.

Instantly the figure reappeared to head me off. I was tired, at any rate; but had I been as fresh as when I rose, I could see it was in vain for me to contend in speed with such an adversary. From trunk to trunk the creature flitted like a deer, running manlike on two legs, but unlike any man that I had ever seen, stooping almost double as it ran. Yet a man it was, in point of fact, a boy, I could no longer be in doubt about that. He was none other than Dhruv.

'You? Idiot. You know how much you make me frightened,' I said.

'What happen?'

'Shut up. What were you doing there?'

'I was doing the same thing that I was doing on the night when you met me along with Shweta.'

'Mean?' I asked very confusingly. He always started talking such useless thing that never entered in my wits.

'Nothing,' he said. 'You just tell what happen and what are you doing here? I think all have already passed away. Right.' He continued firmly.

'Oh! Ya. Actually when you were coming so rapidly from there, I got frightened.'

'You got frightened,' Dhruv started laughing all of a sudden. 'Oh! My God, you thought that some animal was coming. Hahahhaaah' he continued laughing until he founded me a bit fuming.

'Okay sorry. Now let's move,' Dhruv now attuned his Rucksack. Instantly I began to free myself from all thoughts and crawl back again, with what speed and silence I could manage, to the more portion of wood. Dhruv also accompanied me. We were alone for the time, I was happy; as we got some more time and I am sure he was feeling the same. We were just crawling without speaking anything and my heart throbbed more as he held my hand again in order to give me support. All way we moved just like this and thanks to Sandeep who was giving us signal time by time so as to follow the group without any problem. Sandeep and Manish, both were doing their duty of exploring the place very well. Everything was going well. We were well with time.

'So,' I said to start the conversation.

'So, what?'

'U didn't tell?'

'What?' he asked curiously.

'Dhruv is MAD for?' I asked smilingly, but I don't know why he got stopped as such my question burned him up.

'What happen? Why you stopped?'

'Nothing,' he tried to avoid my question again and continued his footsteps slowly.

'If you don't want to tell; no problem, but please talk. I don't want to move on like this.'

Drawing me to his side, 'There is nothing that I can't tell you, but your words always make me remember of someone, someone whom I am not able to forget.'

His words made me almost excited. I was ready to hear my name. Oh yes, Thank God. You can propose me Dhruv. You can. I thought for a while. I could realise shyness on my face. I rolled my eyes. His mouth opened and closed, but no words came out. God, he was looking so cute, I wanted to jump into his arms.

I gave him my best smile. 'May I please know the name?' I asked very curiously, maybe he could even sense that curiousness on my face.

But as he answered '*Shubhi*', my mind moved far away. I turned sideways to let some village women passby, adjusting my Rucksack comfortably.

'Shubhi' word came out from my mouth as a dread but I controlled my feelings. I wasn't filled with that overpowering wave of love that I'd experienced during all those nights at a camp. I had the feeling that Dhruv had told something that was none of my business. Actually, it wasn't a feeling. It was a fact. And I was ready to kill myself. There was no reason to make Dhruv uncomfortable. He could do what he wanted with whomever he wanted.

I was ready to hide my feelings but how couldn't I notice that Dhruv was babbling from nervousness. How cute was that? I was beginning to wonder why I listened to him.

'What are you thinking?' Dhruv asked me in a very low tone.

That was just that. I hadn't been thinking. If I had, I would have hugged him fast, before he had a chance to pull away. But then again, who was I to complicate his life? The idea that someone might have already loved him made me almost ill.

'Hey, Anjali, what are you thinking?' he asked me again.

'Oh! Nothing,' I replied so abruptly as such I came out of any nightmare. 'I was just thinking, who is Shubhi' I continued, feeling all the blood in my body rise to my face. Dhruv lowered his chin, looking up at me sceptically. The same moment, I heard Vivek shouting to warn us from the big rocky area and a small pond in the way. Also I was very much tired. So, though I wasn't interested now, but I held Dhruv's hand and we moved further. Dhruv gripped my fingers very carefully. The whole way

I stared at him as my conscience, my brain, and my heart battled it out over what my next move should be.

The conscience thought I should tell Dhruv that what I was thinking.

The brain told me it was none of my business and that I'd probably forget everything.

And the heart told me just to hug him and wait for the snow to fall. It pounded, prayed everything to be false. Squinting my eyes, I tried to see across the mountains. Sure enough, there was everything, everything natural, and true.

My stomach turned. Dhruv leaned down to elevate me up on a very stony path. I took a step back, but I somehow managed to maintain eye contact and then I pulled myself up straight so that I could handle the weight on my back as it should be. I stopped, and then look a couple of steps in the direction where all were going. My fists were balled up. My knees almost went out. Still I held my ground.

'Keep talking,' I said, all menacing.

'Who's Shubhi?' I asked again in a small voice. I stared at Dhruv, waiting for him to spill and he lowered his chin just slightly, 'my ex-girlfriend'. There was a momentary flash of uneasiness in his eyes. He simply moved ahead of me. While peace was singing all around, I was shaking; however all I could do was hope that he could tell me more about his relationship with Shubhi but he moved quietly, so I followed him absent-mindedly. There was a profound silence. I felt a pang somewhere near my heart, because it made me realize how long it had been since I was thinking that Dhruv loves me, but.... but I think it was not like that.

I can't stay here, I thought for a while but it was when a loud sound of whistle bashed my ears, I understood that we had reached the place. I readjusted my bag which was digging into my shoulders and slowly released it.

We were nearly six hundred feet high from the base camp. It was like a very small vale covered by mountains all around. Tall pine trees were making it more beautiful. Everyone was excited, happy, enjoying the place. Dhruv also released his bag and joined other guys who were picking woods and carrying it over to their lean-to in one quick trip. The light was fading rapidly, and they wanted to get the fire started before it was too dark to see anything. Soon, another group also arrived from some other route and a sort of competition took place between both groups. Everyone got their task. Where Partho, Manish and Vivek pinched the tents, Sandeep, Dhruv and Nitin carefully arranged the tinder and kindling in the pyramid shape and then built a simple box-fire arrangement so as to cook the food, the task for which was given to me and Shilpa.

It was true that I was very much tired and not interested for the program anymore but there was no such option. I wasn't looking for the Dhruv in that dark. I was not searching every face of everybody that sped by me before the first star positioned itself in the sky. Right. And I hadn't even spent an extra ten minutes to clean my face. Pathetic. I was plain.

Dhruv has a girl-friend, I told myself for the millionth time since two hours. *He's a lousy, awful jerk who you wish you'd never met.* Right again. Those dark eyes had been my every thought since that moment at the base camp.

'Get over it, Anjali,' I said aloud as I forced myself to move in a more or less determined manner while smoke from the natural gas smashed my eyes sharply.

Dhruv was not even my type. He was not even smart. But he was very good. He was the only guy who touched my heart. He was really a darling.

'Hey!' I whirled around, ready to be extremely rude to whoever or whatever had gotten at my side.

Instead my breath caught in my lungs. The person was none other than Dhruv, first love of my life. I swallowed what would have been an audible gasp in a girl with less self-control.

Get lost. I knew I could spit out those words in a venomous spurt but then his hands came on my shoulders.

'Can we talk?' he said very calmly. I wanted to say 'no' but I don't know why I followed him to the place under one tree. It was mostly a jumble of rocks with a few clumps of trees stuck here and there. I was very confused, after all, what Dhruv wants to say? But he said nothing for some time and soon silence started killing me.

But suddenly, it was like some philosopher again took birth in his soul.

'Sometimes we don't realize the good fortune we have or we could have because we expect "the packaging" to be different.' Words came out from his lips.

'Ugh?' I sighed. His words were infuriating me. Why can't he be straight? I am not getting him. Such sayings, actually, never entered in my mind but there was something else also; his husky, masculine voice. It held the faintest touch of uncertainty, a hint of masculine pride.

Slowly, he turned.

Her name was Shubhi. She was really the one among all like every guy wants – beautiful, fair and well-shaped. I met her in my first year. She was in IT Deptt. Shubhi, the golden girl with quick decisions, this is how I always called her.

It was the underlying sharpness in his tone that silenced me, even though my heart went into a spin at the prospect of getting to know his life better.

The shock of her proposal was so strong that we shuddered in each other's arm. Even, I was very very surprised.

Like every lover, I also bunked my classes just to see her. Whenever she ate burger in the canteen, goodness, I can never forget the moment. She was really the cutest girl I have ever seen and truly, I had never thought that girl like her could be my girlfriend but with passing time, I realised the opposite. Yes, I didn't deserve her. Guy like me didn't deserve such a darling girl.

I was an idiot. Rather I should say I am an idiot but now it's very late. I seriously loved her from bottom of my heart and I am sure she also did but still I can never forget the moment when two arms came around me and smoothened cheek rubbed against mine. Settling herself, she turned slowly into my arms and tears came then, reaction to her quarrel with me, to her uncertainty as to whether she was doing right in wanting to stay away from me, the tug inside of the child she was intending to deny the guy she loved so deeply, when I wanted her so much.

'Take Care' that were her last words she said while placing the letter in my hand.

Till today, I don't know why she took such a hard decision. Why she didn't give me a chance. I know I was wrong but she could give me one chance. Probably, I didn't deserve the chance also.

So, today I only prayed for her progress, for fulfillment of all her desires and that is the only thing I am MAD for. I am MAD just for her happiness, nothing else. Though I know I can't give her that happiness, but I can make her feel relax by not showing my face to her, as she desired.

Everything got silent again. I was quiet. I stared out at the stars and wrapped my arms around my knees. I realised I was seeing a different side of Dhruv just then. As I attempted to say something but I was struck by a sudden hopeful thought: My Dhruv would never do something wrong. There had to be some sort of explanation. What if –

'Oh' I whispered. My eyes blurred with some tears as I plunged headlong into depression. This couldn't be my life – this couldn't really be happening to me. I pinched myself just to make sure. Oh, yeah, this nightmare came true.

'I thought Dhruv loved me,' I said to myself. I know I loved him…. He was the first guy I ever felt the way about. How could he do this to me?

But he hadn't done anything wrong. He didn't ever say that he loves me. It was me only who thought like this. He was not wrong anymore. He was Dhruv, the guy I'd fallen in love with.

Oh God, I needed to get away from Dhruv, and away from the pile of garbage that my life had turned into. But I think that was not enough so, very courageously, 'but what happened that did despair both of you?' I asked him. 'You can tell me Dhruv,' I continued determinedly.

He shot me an incredulous look and laughed in a way that wasn't funny but he was still silent. I could see the layer of tears under his eyes. The look in his eyes when he turned on me made me shiver, but I forced myself not to back down.

'My love experience is nothing good at all.' He went on while taking out one paper from his wallet and handed over it to me. I was really getting myself worked up imagining the worst.

'What's all this going on?' I thought. I was very much bewildered. I tried to ignore every thought. I was speechless, in fact. It made me so uncomfortable I wanted to run right out of there. For the time being, everything was just a story for me, maybe Dhruv was doing all this just to make me feel jealous but still I wanted to read the paper immediately even though, dark night was a big hurdle. It was like finding out the truth about something when you're better off believing a lie.

I wanted to know the certainty behind their breakup and one thing that I discovered then is that most people really feel dread of imagining something worst to get explored and I was also one of them. Even when I ask for the truth, it's like when you ask someone whether they think the dress you're wearing makes you look fat or if your new haircut makes your ears sticks out – you only want to hear the truth if it's not going to make you feel bad. Or you might have a best friend who says, 'you can tell me anything, no matter how terrible it is,' but you know if you told him about all the times you'd spend with your love and then you had a break-up, surely he/she'd probably hate you.

That's sort of how I felt then. For a minute there, I found I wasn't mad at Dhruv anymore. It was like losing my page in a book and opening it to the wrong page. I didn't know what to say, what to feel. I was too busy feeling sorry for myself. Dhruv, I could tell, was sorry too. Maybe he wasn't as shallow as I'd always thought he was.

What kind of relationship would Dhruv and I have? I wondered. It was still so new and strange that I had a hard time believing the whole episode in the jungle camp wasn't something my mind cooked up. I just closed my eyes in order to relax but a few minutes later Shilpa arrived. Even it was dark, I could sense excitement in her tone.

'Hey guys, food is ready. Come fast.' She said while focusing torch on us.

As words entered our ears, Dhruv got up like a bullet emerging from gun and moved towards the place without saying anything. I'd felt so foolish for the moment but no other option I had, so, Shilpa and I passed this about hundred steps walk together.

'So, how's it going?' Shilpa asked in a very tricky manner. Her tone was like she wants to know some secret.

'What?' I asked astonishingly.

She just smiled. 'You know.'

Her words enhanced my confusion. 'Ask directly *yaar,* what you want to know actually?'

'Did he propose you?' she questioned in a very excited tone and my mind started running in circles. There was no logic to be found in her question. The wind sighed in the tops of the trees that overhung my both sides. Ordinarily I might have been afraid but not tonight. There was nothing in the world that could overcome the misery that clogged my mind. And besides, Shilpa was smiling resolutely along at my side, as if my relationship with Dhruv was just the thing.

'You really make me surprise. Why will he propose me?'

'Because he loves you.'

'And who said you this?' firmly a question rose on my lips.

'Sandeep.'

'What?' creases appeared on my forehead.

'Ya,' Shilpa said in a very surprising manner. 'And why you are so surprised, everyone on the camp knows this.'

For a while, I paused but I held my head as I moved on.

'This place is dead tonight, huh?' I said to myself. Dhruv is saying that he loves Shubhi, and here all are gossiping that he loves me. It looked as though life was trying out different modes for me. Everything was a mess. Other than that, the story was simple. I just need to be quiet. Quiet!

'Yeah. Its better,' I added and took a deep breath.

As I approached I heard a lot of chattering voices. It sounded as though there were a party going on, and I had been a feeling that all were there discussing about me and Dhruv. My heart Started to pound. What if, they were discussing? I didn't know if I could muster up the guts to make everyone listen to me. I glanced from some distance. Sure enough, a bunch of people were just hanging out – sitting around a fire and gossiping.

I sighed and this wasn't actually a big deal. What a big deal was; as I walked in, everyone looked up. I saw a few friends, but a lot more with a strange smile, though no one said anything. I averted my eyes and walked over to my group. Vivek and Partho seemed to be very much excited to eat the food, as it was cooked. Seriously, no one had ever thought that one day we need to dine out like this – in the jungle, under the sky. It was like some reality show had been organised and we were the part of that.

Shilpa started serving food to all, so I found it better to get busy with her. Everyone was ready to have their supper. Though food was not good, but no one could blame Shilpa for this as getting food at such a place was not an easy game.

Dhruv, he was there only, sharing food with Sandeep. I could notice that they were discussing something but words were not clear to me. So, I exhaled slowly. Just one question – 'What are they discussing?'

Oh God, I got stuck in such a trap. It seemed me like I was a billiard bill and all were hitting me to get into a hole. I wanted to change the way the things are but nothing has changed. Cold wind was tuning sharply in my lungs, so I reached my hands out over the flames and raised my knees to my chin.

I stared at the fire for a moment and all of a sudden the letter stuck into my pocket caught my thought immediately. Though I couldn't read it because of dark and now I don't take it out but 'what was there in the letter?' another question pumped in my mind.

'Ugh,' I was dead.

'Listen up.' Sood Sir's eyes scanned the groups. He waited to make sure that he had all our full attention and then while moving all around, 'Life can hand you all sorts of experiences you never thought you'd face,' he continued. 'So why not enjoy the moment fully and have some songs on our lips,' he stoped while cracking a joke, but somehow I seemed to have lost my sense of humour.

Within a minute, it was like a live *Chitrahaar* going on and automatically a sort of competition could be seen among all boys and girls. Everything seemed to me like a movie. Open area, all teenagers, stars twinkling, a girl and a boy in love with each other and people singing kind of romantic songs; tremendous. But it was not a movie.

Soon, the party got over and everyone again got busy in their gossips. Dhruv and Sandeep hung out before crawling into their sleeping bags. I don't know what was cooking between them. 'I must talk to Sandeep' thought rose in my mind. That was when I had come up with his nickname 'Sandy', that's how my neighbour called his doggie. 'Yes, he is really a doggie, how could he say to all that Dhruv loves me. There is definitely something that he knew. I must talk to him,' I said to myself.

That night I paced back and forth across the hard hill while my mind was still struggling with Dhruv's short story and Shilpa's words – '*Did he propose you?*'

That night I glared at the darkness which seemed to be staring at me in an accusatory manner.

The night was apparently rotten as I spent over an hour clenching and unclenching my fists with obvious frustration.

That night I was also hopeful that by the end of tomorrow, Operation *Caught Sandeep Over the Edge* was going to be over and done.

Time went by quickly. I wondered why they had set alarms on their cell phones. I hadn't slept properly. My body was aching. On the other hand, the days flew by. Wednesday blurred into Thursday, this transformed into Friday and so on.

'Oh, No,' again alarm tones knocked me along with somebody's voice. 'Hey Shilpa, Anjali, Swati wakeup *yaar*, we have to leave within fifteen minutes and everything needs to be packed.' Mightbe it was Mandeep's voice.

'*Fuck,*' I groaned while rubbing my eyes. It was still very dark but I could hear the voice of guys, loading their things.

Momentarily, everything got packed in a panic. I couldn't help myself as we had to go back to the base camp. Truly saying, descending on the hill was tougher as compared to climb the same, particularly it was very risky due to dark. Every step must be kept with care. There was an order of being along with the group, however, I was left behind, you know why, because I was playing a very good role of being a Sood Sir's tortoise. But I was not alone. I could notice one figure carrying Rucksack, covering me. I made sure that he was Dhruv only, though we didn't talk. He also held my hand sometimes. I clasped the long fingers of his hand and heaved myself onto the rock. Sometimes, he even moved ahead of me in order to clear the path but no words interchanged between us. At least no words were spoken out loud. I was having an unpleasant one-way conversation with the back of Dhruv's head as I struggled to keep my foot carefully. *You're cute. You're worthless human being. You're everything to me. No you're nothing to me.* The mental babbling went on and on.

As time passed, I became less and less aware of the triumph of light over dark. I just followed the path Dhruv showed me. Although I could hear Vivek and Partho yelling over us, I couldn't decipher exactly what they were saying – which was probably the best. Guilty feeling of being slow was building at a rapid rate. Still, it was what my heart had wanted…right?

He turned around to glance at me one more time, which prompted me to jerk my head back to other direction. If Dhruv knew I took every opportunity to stare at him, he might become just the least bit suspicious of my feelings, which were having no values by then. Mightbe these feelings had no importance before Shubhi. Mightbe my presence will also have no value before her. But still there was one thing in my mind, Operation – *Caught Sandeep* was to be done and still I could hope for something.

Everyone was free for the day as from tomorrow onwards we had to depart for trekking. I shrugged and glanced at my watch, as if there were a thousand places I would rather be. But *Gosh*! In any case, I didn't forget that it was our last day at base camp and for next five days we would rarely get any chance of bathing, so I bathed, however the water was extremely cold. It seemed that I would definitely get froze there only, if I stayed there for some more seconds.

I felt the rush of homesickness as I found myself lonely, although it was my decision only as I wanted to be alone for some time. So I just laid down at the side of River *Asi Ganga*.

Passing that time seemed very difficult. For that reason, I couldn't help but threw stones in the water; noticed the pine trees, lined unmannerly on the hill, but then only the letter stuck into my pocket caught my attention immediately. I took out a small white square and unfolded it with care one might show to his final semester question paper. I almost didn't want to read the words Shubhi had written.

Right now, poised before her scrawling hand-writing, the possibilities were endless but I read it, read it as slowly as possible.

Dear Dhruv,

Happy Birthday. So, how was the party last night? I have heard a lot about hostel parties, especially in boy's hostel – Bang! Bang! Dancing, liquor, gossips, totally Hungama!! And the one definitely needs to be like Hungama; after all it's our final year. I know you have enjoyed a lot with all your friends – Vipin, Nishant, Ravinder, Vinay, Arjun and ya, that short guy, Sneha's boy friend, who gave you lot of birthday bumps, ya right - Nikhil. What? How I know? Actually, I used to talk to Sneha about you; after all she lives just next to my room only.

Oh, ya thanks for the scarf. I know, today I should give you something but actually I was confused. I went to the market but nothing came into my mind.

I wish you won't mind. I am not like you after all; everything you touch turns to something special. You know you're genius Dhruv. Me, no I am not. How can I be dear? How can a mistress be genius?

No, No, No, No, No, don't broaden your eyes. Don't be like an owl. Today is your birthday dear. Perhaps, some whisky bottles will be spared and again you will like to declare me as your mistress, as you did last night.

You were right; I must warn Sneha about Nikhil. He is truly a bastard.

You know, I was in tenth grade, when one boy at my tuition runs his hand on my back. Since that day, I hated all boys but today, I am not able to use word "HATE" for you. It seemed irrelevant, not only because what you did, but also because I love you. Maybe that not sounds neat to you but it's a truth that I loved you more than anyone else.

Well, I will not take more of your time. It's all over. I love you very much Dhruv, but I think I can't continue with you now. So, please don't call me, if you really want your mistress to be happy.

And thanks again for the scarf. It will always remind me the mistake I did.

Shubhi hadn't signed the note. She didn't need to. I read and re-read the letter a dozen of times, my heart pounding so fast, I thought I might have a heart attack.

I was almost lost in myself. *How could Dhruv do this? Did he really do that? What's going on actually?* Frequently such stuffs pumped into my mind. Half of my mind didn't want to believe it but another half was opposing the same.

Oh God! How could he say such words for any girl? No, I don't want to think all this. I don't want to read this letter. I crumpled up the piece of loose paper, determined to throw the letter away and expel its contents from my mind forever.

Inhale. Exhale. I think Sood Sir's exercise was affecting me very much. Inhale. Exhale. Why was I lying to myself? This letter was going nowhere but straight into my pocket. I quickly decrumpled the precious piece of paper and smoothened it as much as possible. Then I carefully folded it into a small square and stuck it into the front-left pocket of my jeans.

While my head was already burning with temper, hot sun was too roasting it very sincerely and then only my eyes caught Sandeep carrying few chairs to the tent and the thought of Operation again hit me. Mightbe the guys were planning something but that couldn't change my frame of mind, my operation. I'd completely forgotten that I'd promised myself that I would talk to Sandeep regarding everything going on.

'But do I still need to know anything now? No... Yes... No... Mightbe... oh yes... I still want to talk to him,' my heart conveyed the message steadfastly. So, I waved Sandeep with a yell twice. And I couldn't help again but notice the foot of Sandeep approaching towards me. Oh man, my heartbeat thumped heavily as he approached me.

Now....what was I going to do?

I had no idea from where I should start but I knew that nothing would stop me today to know what I wanted to know.

'I will definitely catch him,' I promised. 'I mean, I'll ask him,' I amended in a chillier voice.

All right, so it had taken a few seconds, but my cool had kicked back in. The old Anjali was lurking somewhere inside me. I just had to find her before Sandeep reached to me, when

I had a feeling that those dark black eyes would be looking at me with a gaze.

'Hi Anjali,' Sandeep said very calmly.

'Hi.' Mightbe he had noticed some tightness in my tone.

'Ya say, what happen?' His so calm tone was making me freak and enhancing the strain over my mind.

'I want to talk to you.'

'Regarding what?'

'Regarding Dhruv,' I replied as softly as possible. Sandeep got silent for a while and then nodded. 'Okay.'

'You are his good friend, right'

'Ya.'

'So, obviously you know everything about him.'

'Maybe, yes. But what you wana know,' he asked safely.

'Do you know about his and Shubhi's relationship?' His quick glance assured me that my words hit him flatly.

'Yes,' he said serenely. 'Dhruv and Shubhi had been together forever,' he continued. 'They were like, the best couple'.

'Oh,' I whispered while plunging headlong back into depression.

'He loved Shubhi from the bottom of his heart.'

'Oh, ya that's why only he said such things about her to his friends. You know he's not less than any jerk; he's a ---- a ---- I mean how could he say such things about Shubhi,' I said solidly with anger in my eyes. 'And you; you are more than a jerk; you are escalating a rumour that he loves me.' I yelled once again, slamming my fists down on the rock. I don't know what happened to me suddenly.

'What?' Sandeep shouted so heavily, it seemed like my heartbeat got stop for a fraction of seconds.

'Hello Miss Anjali, firstly please reduce your volume along with such a temper. It is infuriating me,' he continued.

He got quiet for what felt like an hour but was probably more like ten seconds. 'You know some guys are just extremely Idiots and Dhruv is the leader of those guys. And you know why, because he loves you – loves you a lot.' His words almost shivered me. This was not the response I had expected. Or maybe it was. Maybe that was exactly I had allowed myself to ask the question. But I definitely hadn't anticipated the sincerity that I heard in his voice.

'It's true that he was in relationship with Shubhi. He even misses her a lot and he had also done a big mistake as you very well know. But there is also one more truth you should know, that Shubhi is not in his life now and he has a right to love again. If you have a breakup, it doesn't mean that you can't welcome love in your life again, right.' Sandeep's words entered in my mind like a missile. He was right. Every Human being has a right to love again.

'You know Anjali,' he continued very softly, 'you are not as smart as you are thinking. You are only viewing one side of the coin. How can you ignore one more reality that he didn't hide anything from you. He confessed everything on his own because he is truly embarrassed for what he had done. Though he had one more option, he could hide everything from you and I am sure you would never know anything. But he told you everything, because he loves you and he wants to have a truthful relationship with you. Not like any jerk, understand.'

I looked at Sandeep and dropped down my legs into the water. He seemed to be very angry but his words had a calming effect on me. I let out a shaky sigh. But as I glanced up at him again, I found him walking out of my view. His speed was surely intimating me his anger. I was virtually clean bowled. My stomach twisted in nauseating turns at the mere thought of eliminating Dhruv from my life. But how could I possibly do that?

I couldn't believe that just a few days ago I'd been under the illusion that Dhruv is simply in love with me. But after that I'd also managed to get bad things, make myself sick and stay up all night worrying about him and Shubhi. And now, I was realising how true my illusion was.

Dhruv loves me. OMG, he loves me. I am sure if Sandeep was there by that time he could analyze how deeply I was dying for Dhruv. 'Sandeep was right. Every human has a right to love and whatever he did, he did it by mistake. Shubhi was only his past but now I am his present. He loves me. Yes, he loves me.' I said to myself.

'*But?*' I hated my voice.

'But what to do now?' The question was simple, but it brought tautness on my face.

Oh, no. Oh God, I wanted him to know exactly how I felt. I wanted him to know that I love him, there was no way I could stop. He means everything to me. 'Yes' I was almost convincing myself. I wanted him to be mine. I love him. Such thoughts trapped me for a while. So, I closed my eyes, hoping to escape the thoughts that chased around my head, but it was no use. Besides, I couldn't stop seeing Dhruv in my mind. I kept hearing his voice too. I imagined him saying '*I love you Anjali. Will you marry me?*'

He stared at me for a long moment, his dark eyes were thoughtful. I was glad that he was looking at me. I felt his eyes on me even after I turned my eyes. I knew he was probably waiting for me to hand him over Shubhi's letter. But still it was good to just sitting there, watched by him and waiting for Sood Sir, not knowing what he would say now.

'What is the program for today's eve?' I heard the feminine voice from behind asking the question to Amandeep, sitting on my left.

'Don't know,' he replied smartly with a gesture and conversation got over. But a kind of *chutter-putter* was still in the business.

Where I was searching my destiny, some were laughing, some talking, and some having snapshots and likewise some were viewing beauty around them. *Ya, Dhruv was still watching me.* I smiled with that thought.

'Listen' then only Sood Sir's voice approached all. 'So how are you?' he continued.

'Good Sir,' voices rose.

'Enjoying?' his voice raised in exciting manner.

'Yes Sir,' even we were louder than before. Everyone could feel the excitement in each other's tone. I could even sense the energising effect of last five days on every face.

'So, ready for what you have come,' he continued while accelerating the spirits in all. Seriously, Sood Sir is a very good leader. He actually deserves to be the best. I felt the same for the moment.

'Yes Sir.'

'Okay, Good. It's really nice to see all of you so excited and fresh. So, get ready as tomorrow we are going to leave the Base camp and move towards our goal. And our first Milestone will be '*Bhebra*', okay.'

Everyone nodded smilingly with a few 'Yes Sir' voices.

'And don't forget the only rule of this trekking – everyone should be with his/her group.'

'Yes Sir.' Again a togetherness could be seen in all voices.

A kind of power was rising in all. Everyone was in hurry to move, to reach the top. Even I was feeling the same power now. I could hardly feel any tension. Thought of Dhruv's love for me was giving me a sort of magical power. My homesickness seemed to be flown away. My body pain seemed to be evaporated. My legs wanted to run and run and run and to be in his arms. I wanted to be with him.

Later that night, I was not able to sleep. I smiled in relief. It looked like we could be together in this sublime Himalayas. I wanted to talk to him, though I was also confused that how should I start. Different thoughts were arising in my mind – *When will he propose me? How could I intimate him about my feelings? Should I start the conversation or let leave everything on him?* And then while boxing with my brain I found a simple solution. Let's leave everything on time – the best solution ever for any human, perhaps to compromise with the state, he/she is passing by. But I liked it that way – or so I was told myself. Our relationship was somehow safe now, no surprises.

Surprises make me nervous, actually. So again I imagined him saying the same '*I love you Anjali. Will you marry me please?*' and closed my eyes. And this was the only day when I understood that not only Dhruv but I was also a fool, you know why, because – *I was also in love.*

Chapter 3

Love @ 13,500 ft

The actual trek starts from Sangamchatti, about 5 kms from the Base Camp. All started in a jeep towards Sangamchatti around eight in the morning. And Dhruv, leaned back, closed his eyes, and tilted his face up towards the roof of the jeep, feeling as though all energy had been drained out of him. He was really getting warmed up now. The experience was turning from nerve-racking to empowering to strangely real.

'*Excuse me,*' a sudden sweet voice moved in his ear.

His eyes popped open, and he was like on the seventh cloud. Just the thought of Anjali was enough to recharge his system and here she was approaching him with a smile. She looked exceedingly elegant, and although her face was a little serious as she concentrated on her hairs while she sat by his side. Very soon, Vivek, Partho, Sandeep, Nitin and Shilpa also joined in and the driver shut the door from outside. During this small journey their bodies were just inches apart. It seemed that Dhruv's strain started to slip away. Exactly.

It took only ten minutes to reach the place. Gradually, other jeeps also arrived and all got bunched as per their group. Sangamchatti, about 4500 ft. above the sea level, was their starting point. The place has some small *dhabas* and tea stalls. In his mind's eye, Dhruv could see what Anjali was seeing. The trail crosses the bridge over *Asi Ganga* and goes towards *Bhebra*. 'It seemed very much exciting' thought Anjali. Maybe. Or maybe it was something different, something that would test her, push her own limits. She leaned over and picked up a thick stick, she found at some side of the road. And the next thing she knew that all were moving towards the target.

The first run seemed endless. It took them all over the side of hills, which seemed to be so dangerous that a single mistake in keeping a foot could make you fall into the depths. The route actually followed the long path that led past few bushy areas, one or two villages, and some local people were passing by along with their mules. Far away, the pattern of terrace farming could be seen with clouds kissing the top of hills and adjacently, Dhruv could be found holding the hands of Anjali and passing the tricky Himalayan range.

The walk was conducted in silence. Dhruv was actually very much stressed. The trouble is, he thought with sorrow, that Anjali doesn't seemed to love him, especially after acknowledging his past and his blunders. Though he also expected that she never liked him as the day when Anjali's declaration '*If you guys think that I am in love, then please, never think of this*' flashbacked in his mind. There was a puzzled expression on his face.

Had he made a terrible mistake? Events until now had carried him through; there had been no time to think, let alone to doubt. How little he knew about Anjali. He did not even know her likes and dislikes, and as usual of his idiotic nature, he had told her everything about him. '*Why would a girl like a guy who disreputes that girl. What happen if he is helping her entire way, if he will not be there, some other guy will definitely play the same part. And even Anjali is such a darling that any guy would be ready to hold her hands. Who is he in any case?'* thought flowed in his mind. He looked frazzled and unclean.

If only they could have fallen straight into each other's arms and made love, free of inhibitions and restraint, the act itself would have forged an intimate link which would have bound them so closely, every bone and fiber of their being would have melded together, breaking through all barriers and making them one.

If only Dhruv would, then Anjali would have relaxed, too. Her limbs would have lost their tension, her lips would have smiled, her eyes might even, despite the lingering poison of Dhruv's claims, have whispered, '*love me*'.

But again the trouble was same – Dhruv had its own imagination, own thoughts and own doubts. He was wrong about only one thing – Anjali's feelings towards him.

And Anjali, she couldn't have asked about more romantic atmosphere. The cold air aeas freshening their lungs, open sky welcoming them, beautiful mountain carrying them in its arms and Dhruv holding her hand behaving like a husband, a lover, distracting her from the toughness she could feel while trekking such a tricky route. Anjali was getting lost in a sea of uncountable emotion. She wanted him, needed him more than she had ever needed him before. He was chasing away all her pain with his customary ease and Anjali was aware of her dependence on him resurfacing with every passing moment. There seemed to be nothing more to say. '*It is all very exciting!*' she thought. She gave a little sigh which was almost one of happiness. And then she recalled the time when Dhruv said '*You are beautiful*' to her and a smile appeared on her face.

It was their fourth hour on the trek after having a hot Maggie and omelets in the way. The sunlight was almost gone in the area. Dhruv had held Anjali's hand almost the whole way from Sangamchatti to the place while both too had their Rucksacks on their back. They moved slowly along, down the straight road pointing into the shady place. And now it was almost hundredth time when Anjali relaxed on the rock and Sood Sir, walking by, saw them and circled back to wave and indicate them their target a few hundred steps away.

But this time, a noise of waterfall calmed their ears. Cold air enriched their lungs. It seemed like some waves of excitement passed from Anjali's body.

'*Thank God*' Sood Sir's indication and small huts in view made her almost relaxed while Dhruv hold her hands again and moved, watching their first milestone, watching the landscape where they have to spend a night.

Truly saying the time was as much terrific after knowing that all have to spend their night in the huts, it was as much terrible also after acknowledging the fact that for further days no toilets were available. Even for a shit one has to go in an open area with the provided axe and burrow the waste underground.

Very optimistically, a new kind of experience was waiting for all.

Bhebra was there, 7500 ft. above sea level, small and a very nice place hidden on the lap of Himalayas. An undersized waterfall was enhancing the loveliness of the area. The place was actually very quiet; there was no one around as well, except a few huts and an old man with a small shop of eatables like Maggie or Cold Drinks.

Surprisingly, It was around 17:30 hrs only when the Sun had slipped behind the mountains and the darkness seemed to swallow the part very slowly. Moonlight poured through the hut windows. Mountains seemed to be black. Everyone felt the evening chill in their bones. There had already been chill for four nights this week and now it was another, so having a cup of tea was a wonderful idea.

Finishing their cup of tea all sat back, chattered, tittle-tattled and wondered what to do next. Suddenly all heard a whistle. It was Nishit.

'Come on,' he said. 'Let's play Truth and Dare.'

Wave of interest flowed in all. Some girls hesitated, thinking of all the reasons why they shouldn't play but on tenterhooks, everyone circled around the row of two tables, a few torches hanging on the roof of small shed.

'Hey *Sangwan*, spin the bottle yaar,' Nishit's voice rose excitingly.

For a moment life seemed to be very fast to all as such something, very strong was pulling them towards it. Some invisible power was attracting them like they were on a mission. But instead of the body pain, the long hectic trek which hurt their foot, all were laughing, sounding great, excited, ready to discover their new world.

'Hey Anshu it's you, say… Truth or Dare,' Sangwan said curiously.

'Truth,' a very confident voice was coming from there.

For a moment all mind went into a deep thought.

'Okay...Okay… Let me ask,' Amandeep said. Flavour of the game arrested all in a while.

'Among all the guys present here, who will you like to date?'

'What? What kind of question is this?'

'Just say yaar, it's a game only. If you have to choose someone then who will be that guy,' Amandeep said again.

'Okay… Okay... Hmmm… *Anshuman,*' Anshu replied with a deep thought.

A noise of claps echoed all around.

'Hey wait. Wait. Let me also clear one thing. I said his name because he is my very good friend. Don't take it like anything else. Okay,' Anshu continued.

'Ya' everyone said and smiled while Sangwan was ready for another spin.

The game goes on one by one. Ms Poonam, the only lady instructor, also joined the group. All were enjoying. Dhruv and Anjali had also found themselves becoming more and more placid. Shilpa's beautiful voice made the moment more memorable. Nishit's jokes, Dwarka's stupidity made everyone laugh. The temperature goes on decreasing making the evening colder and then another spin took action and the bottle stopped pointing towards Dhruv.

'Hey Dhruv. Truth or Dare,' Amandeep asked swiftly.

'Truth.'

'May I ask please,' Shilpa interrupted curiously. It seemed like she was waiting from a long time for the moment.

'Dhruv, please don't mind. But do you like Anjali?' words banged in swiftly.

Everyone got surprised. For an instant, question shined in every eye.

Raising her head, Anjali looked around. Her arms fell to her side with such a sudden question. She didn't expect this. She appeared confused and shocked but Inside, she was smiling, an honest smile so full of hope it made her think of the princess waiting for the prince who will kiss her and discharge her from the curse of being a frog.

But for Dhruv everything seemed like a crash took place. Outside he appeared very serene and mature. Inside, he was hamburger. He felt like the broken watch. He felt smashed and wrecked. He felt like a goat who had been corralled and slaughtered and all ground up. He closed his eyes, and as if the words he imagined Anjali saying to him –

You Idiot you like me. You duffer, how could a guy like you love any girl. How dare you think that any girl can live her life with you? Mind it okay and never dare the same again.

'Mind it okay and never dare the same again. Mind it okay and never dare the same again...' words echoed in his mind and a sudden reply '*No*' from his mouth filled Anjali's heart with tears.

For a few minutes, the game goes on. No one reacted on the situation. Anjali tried to be normal but the truth was she seemed to shrink in on herself. She felt almost tricked by fate. Time passed slowly. Everything traumatised again. All got busy in their activities. Where some were ready with an axe, some were ready to sleep. But Anjali hesitated in the doorway. She seemed to be looking at Dhruv, sitting aside of the fire along with some guys. She must have thrown water on the fire but she switched off her torch. Thinking of Dhruv, of their first meeting, of Sandeep's words, broke something deep inside. All her enthusiasm seemed to be flown away.

'This guy could make a decision of his own that would have nothing to do with what she felt and hoped. He could tear her in two – a second time. He doesn't love me' thought of losing her first love made her almost scared.

She touched the door and paused, holding the doorframe, now staring up at the moon. Her eyes swept the black mountains, the dark cedars, the noise of water flowing in the river. She seemed to listen, and then she cupped her hands around her face.

Right away, Dhruv was unaware of the situation, unaware of Anjali's feelings that he shattered unintentionally. His eyes were full of water without remembering the smell of that night, without remembering an unbearable pain he felt in his thighs. Here it came again: the thoughts, the feelings, and the longing. Sitting there at side of fire, speaking of professional and personal life, all he could think of Anjali. Of where she was right now, how she felt when she read the letter.

In actual, he wanted to get home fast. He wanted to be with his mother. He wanted to be away from the shadow of Anjali. Yes, the guy who was waiting for the best time for exposing his feelings now wanted to run away from his own promise of admitting love.

'He might get any chance but now Shilpa's question closed that door also' he thought. '*What will she think of me? Yes, she will laugh at me, definitely all girls will make fun of me. Did she know how much I love her? She did not even return Shubhi's letter. May be she had shown the same to all girls. I am an Idiot. I am Stupid. No, in fact I am a loser,'* different thoughts arose in his mind.

He hoped she didn't have a lover. He tensed up, thinking about it. His head was aching. And all he'd been able to think about loving Anjali in dreams only.

But the feeling contained other elements – not linked to guilt of any kind – as well. Dhruv couldn't get her lips, her sweet smile out of his mind. He was absorbed and obsessed with it, like a boy who'd held a girl for the first time.

Truthfully, it was madness and he couldn't get rid of it.

Life, sometimes play like Hide-and-Seek with us. Our thoughts only seemed to be our great enemies. Our power seemed to be stranger. Others' faults seem to be ours. Likewise dreams everything seems false.

For a phase we forget that life is actually not less than any beautiful song. It never sends disease, accident or suffering. It holds no grudge against you. It never condemns you. It does not judge you. It never punishes. We are the only one, who brings these things on ourselves by our own negative destructive thinking. There is nothing good or bad, but thinking makes it so. People punish themselves by their false thinking. Our thoughts are very creative and they create their own misery. Actually life heals a cut on our hand. It forgives us if we burn our finger. It restores the part to wholeness. But we move on like stupid making compromises with our situations. We agree to live our life on false attitude and forget that all our opinions are our own formation.

And the same was happening with Dhruv and Anjali that day. Both were walking separately with two different reasons. Neither of them said any word, nor did they exchange any view. The mental agony they went through at that time was terrible. Both were like sandwiched between past and future and Dhruv started to feel that he was wasting his time if nothing happened.

'It is a long but an easy walk' Mr Sood now had to motivate all. Each one was made to experience their strength and weakness. Almost all apprehensions and fears were removed from many and complete trust developed in each other. Now again, team had to plan, organize and lead from start to finish. Maggie point at *Kacheru* (6.5 km) from *Bhebra* was going to be their first landmark for the *Dodital* and both Dhruv and Anjali not passed even a look till the point. Both felt quite alone.

Although the distance from Bhebra to Dodital was around 14 km, but for a moment life seemed to be very slow. However, with some short cuts; it was really fun. One could glimpse the snow-capped mountains in the way.

The whole route was through the forests of mainly Oak and Rhododendron. After passing *Kacheru* there was a small settlement called *Majhi* about 9 km from Bhebra and 2.5 kms from Kacheru. There were also some small *dhabas* at the place but most of them were closed because of winter. Starting from early morning, till two in afternoon, moving like donkeys, with your foot aching, just having one plate of Maggie and some water in the stomach, was not an easy job. So, Majhi was a great place both to rest your buttocks and having a lunch. In point of fact, where some were enjoying the trip, some were like they were dumped in to the hell.

'Oh, God. Life had never been this complicated to me. I am dying. Please give me water' Anjali's voice could be heard easily. She was in a mess, and she had no one to turn to. At least no one in this place. She was clearly sick of hearing about Dhruv and her gossips. She pushed her way through the as-per-usual packed Rucksack very toughly and still 5 kms were left. Thought in itself was slaughtering her. It seemed that open sky, beautiful mountains, fresh air, all had lost its value for her.

Sandeep understood what's all going. In fact, all were aware of the story setting up there. He went out of his way to create a friendly atmosphere as initially some misunderstanding had crept up which he did not like to continue. It was very important from his side.

'Hey, what Happen?' Sandeep walked in with a smile. 'Is everything Okay?' he continued.

'Nothing, just getting very much tired.' Anjali replied unenthusiastically.

Sandeep didn't bother asking if she was sure or relaxed and suddenly he started laughing. His reaction made her little angry and confused on another part. In her dark brown jacket, she stood like a statue.

'Why are you laughing?' she asked with creases on her forehead.

'Nothing,' Sandeep replied with a laugh.

'I said, why are you laughing?' Sandeep could sense anger rising in her eyes.

'Do you ever hear the story of an apple tree?'

'Which one?'

'The Law of Seed.'

'No.'

'Okay. Let me tell you,' Sandeep said.

Take a look at an apple tree. There might be five hundred apples on the tree, but each apple has just ten seeds. That's a lot of seeds!

We might ask, 'why would you need so many seeds to grow just a few more apple trees?'

Nature has something to teach us here. It's telling us: 'Not all seeds grow. In life, most seeds never grow. So if you really want to make something happen, you had better try more than once.' He finished his speech.

'But why are you telling this to me?' Anjali inquired.

Sandeep smiled again. 'This might mean: You'll attend twenty interviews to get one job. You'll interview forty people to find one good employee. You'll talk to fifty people to sell one book, one car, or one radio. And you might meet a hundred people just to find special one in your life.' He finished while giving pressure to his last line.

Anjali understood what Sandeep wants to say.

'Is your mind at its place?'

'Yes, but I think not yours. Why are you hiding your love?'

'What? You just do your work. Okay. I don't love him. Can't you see that we are not even going together?' Anjali said while avoiding eye to eye contact with him.

'Ya I can see. But I can also see two Idiots hiding their love from each other.'

'You have completely gone mad. Perhaps you forget that I have told you – I don't love him. You heard – I don't love him.' She glanced at him, raised a brow in frustration.

'Perhaps you forget that a guy here is looking for you from the first day, a guy here is caring for you at every moment, a guy here is taking your snaps at every pose he could, a guy is here who does not sleep before gossiping about you.' Anjali could still sense a smile on his face like he was laughing at her.

Her brows rose higher; she could see the thoughts – the speculation – whirling through his mind.

'Mightbe you forget that last night your that guy only declared – that he doesn't love me. Right.'

'Ya, that's because he thinks that you hate him.'

'What?'

'Yes.' And he just moved from the place.

'Hey where are you going?'

'I think we have to reach Dodital today. Hope you have not forget this.'

'May I come with you?'

'Why not, after all we are a team.'

From Majhi, the trail became a little narrower. Dodital was around 5 km from the place. It was a complete forest trek. The air beneath the trees was silent, still. Path seemed like any movie scene; dry yellow leaves fallen and long trees at both side of the route. Presence of mountain monkeys frightened most of the girls. For a moment it seemed that one has lost the path but they were on the right trek. Anjali calmed as she found all others coming the same way.

'So, you didn't tell me?' she said.

'What?'

'Why he thinks that I hate him?'

'Because you don't love him.'

'Who said?'

'Mean. You only said – that day at camp.'

Anjali understood till now that Sandeep had caught her lies and feelings.

'But that doesn't mean that I hate him. He is a good friend. If he thinks so because of those words, it's his stupidity.'

'Mean you are saying that he should say yes, yesterday.'

Anjali felt herself almost trapped.

'No, I mean, is this the only reason he thinks that I hate him.'

'He thinks that you hate him for the mistake he committed with Shubhi. You didn't even return him Shubhi's letter. According to him, why a girl would will love him when he disrespected another.'

'Okay.'

'And that's why he said 'No', not because he don't love you.'

It was like a great shock to Anjali. Something inside her physically shook. She held his gaze for a long moment, finally got the courage to ask, 'Are you sure?'

'Yes, and I am also sure for one more thing.'

'And what's that?'

'That Anjali is also in same pool of love, feeling same for him.'

She shook her head down with uncertainty to confess. She might as well call it by its real name; love was what it had to be – there was no longer any point to Sandeep doubting that. It was there, between them, almost tangible, never truly absent.

'Wow!' Sudden words from Sandeep's lips again mystified Anjali and she raised her brows.

There is always some amount of joy when one reaches the destination. Be it on any tour. Of course, the other part was sheer curiosity, that Sandeep was very much eager. He wanted to explore the area, so he moved faster.

'Hey, just tell me one more thing,' Anjali said firmly.

'What?'

'If you think that I also love him, then why you don't make your friend understand 'The Law of Seed."

'You know, you have a point, but I can't make him understand, firstly because he doesn't like anyone else to interrupt in his matter and secondly because he only told me this apple story.' And with such a sweet lie Sandeep finally moved on.

Anjali was astonished. The emotional risk she faced till now had just decreased. She breathed in deeply. She had to believe everything Sandeep told – there was no longer any option.

After a moment she also stepped towards *Dodital*, awesome place at 10,800 ft. Dhruv had already reached there an hour ago. Anjali found him relaxing in a big lawn type area, to the side was a lake full of rare fish Trout or *Dodi* (in the local language) from which the lake gets its name. The place actually believed to be the birth place of Lord Ganesha as the lake was believed to be the one where mother *Parvati* formed a statue of Lord Ganesha while bathing. There was also a small temple of Lord Ganesha near the lake. On the far end of the lake, was a trail going further towards Darwa Top which is en route Yamnotri.

By the time, everyone reached and pitched the tents, it was late afternoon. There was also couple of small *dhabas* and tea shops, one of which was open.

So, halfway cross Anjali moved to the shop and ordered for a Maggie, her stomach was demanding firmly. She saw Dhruv there, leisurely roaming with Sandeep. And her mind turned determinedly to the topic.

Him… and… her. Together.

An almost unbelievable thought, according to her. But actually, she'd learned the answer. Quite possibly too well.

Smilingly, she looked down to her palm. Was she truly considering marrying Dhruv?

Yes.

Why?

Not because she loves him. While that aspect was all very nice, she understood that Dhruv also loves him. She couldn't imagine even now, even with him – to be alone. It was that elusive something that had grown between them that had added definitive weight and influenced her so strongly. It was as if she was exploring something, some unknown landscape between them, all on personal dare. She had not an ounce of fear. Now, she was eager and sure of him, sharing the moment even though she didn't know what would come. On balance, if she didn't find him, she would have the satisfaction of knowing that she had tried regardless of any cost to her heart. So, she was ready to propose Dhruv on her own.

And Dhruv, how he felt.

He was still in that same false impression – and by the time all his remaining confidence also dropped down. Despite the fact that he wanted her with an urgency that stole his breath, Anjali's today's strange response kicked off all his thoughts.

'So, how's everything going?' Sandeep tried to enquire.

'It's really cold.'

'I am not ensuring about outside temperature, I am asking about inner one.'

'Mean?'

Suddenly Sandeep smiled. His reaction almost confuses Dhruv.

'What happen? Why are you smiling?' He asked with creases on his forehead.

'Nothing,' Sandeep replied with a laugh.

'Why are you laughing?'

'Do you ever hear the story of an apple tree?' he continued while laughing.

'Which one?'

'The Law of Seed.'

'No.'

'Okay. Let me tell you,' Sandeep said.

Take a look at an apple tree. There might be five hundred apples on the tree, but each apple has just ten seeds. That's a lot of seeds!

We might ask, 'why would you need so many seeds to grow just a few more apple trees?'

Nature has something to teach us here. It's telling us: 'Not all seeds grow. In life, most seeds never grow. So if you really want to make something happen, you had better try more than once.' He terminated.

'But why are you telling this to me?' Dhruv inquired.

Sandeep smiled again. 'This might mean: You'll attend twenty interviews to get one job. You'll interview forty people to find one good employee. You'll talk to fifty people to sell one book, one car, or one radio. And you might meet a hundred people just to find special one in your life.' He finished while giving pressure to his last line.

Dhruv understood what Sandeep wants to say.

'You are talking about Anjali. Right?' Dhruv enquired.

'Yes.'

'So, what do you want?'

'I want that guy who always tries to learn something from his surroundings now to teach the lesson of love to all. I want that guy who promised himself for admitting his love to do the same. I want you to propose her. You're always telling us not to give up, no matter what. How come you're not taking your advice?'

'Let's leave the topic *yaar*. Nobody takes their own advice. If everybody did, there'd be no one left to give it to. And all this love, romance, heart; these words are not meant for me. Whom I will propose, her, who doesn't even want to go with me.'

'Who said?'

'Can't you see her reaction today?'

'Why didn't you call her?'

'Because I know she didn't like me, I told you several times.'

'But did she tell you?'

'What?'

'That she hates you.'

'No.'

'Then?'

'What do you mean by then?'

'I mean, when she never says that she hates you, however she reacted today, she never did the same earlier. She always travelled with you. Then, how can you say that she hates you.'

'You want to say that she loves me. Right.'

'I didn't say that.'

'Then, what do you mean by all this?'

'I mean she doesn't hate you.'

'But she doesn't love me either.'

'I didn't say that also.'

'She doesn't hate me. She doesn't love me. Can you please set to one thing?'

'Ya.'

'What?'

'That she doesn't hate you.'

Dhruv got irritated. He was hard, aching.

'See Dhruv, please don't get angry. I am your friend. Just tell me one thing sincerely. Please,' Sandeep said very calmly.

'Okay ask.' Dhruv tried to calm down.

'How is this place where you are standing?'

'Beautiful.'

'Okay mightbe very soon, the place will be covered by snow, then?'

'Then also it will be beautiful.'

'Okay. You mean, either it will be covered by snow or not, the fact is that place is beautiful. Right?'

Dhruv nodded.

'Then, why it matters that either she loves you or not, the fact is that you love her and your love is pure and beautiful. So just propose her and leave everything on time.'

Dhruv understood everything very well. It's just like his battery got charged.

'Hey Sandeep, you are right. Why should I worry if she hates me or loves me? The fact is that I love her and it's her decision either she wants to accept me or not.'

'That's what I want to make you understand.'

'Thanks bro, let me propose her now only.'

'Hey, wait..., wait... no need to hurry. Propose her tomorrow at Darwa Top.'

'Ya good Idea.' Dhruv's face seemed to be enhanced by a sudden happiness. It seemed like Sandeep had charged him with a battery.

Twenty minutes later, all were pulled into the lawn. A bonfire program was to be organised so all were excited. It was a tradition, called the bonfire of triumph, and as Mr Sood had explained it happened on the night before everyone moved towards their final goal. The temperature was decreasing slowly. It might be about six degrees when Mr Sood blazed the woods. And as the evening progressed, weather got cleared and the sky was full of millions and millions of stars.

'Your first real test was Dodital and you all passed,' Mr Sood told all. 'Before coming here, many of you may be scared of height. Some of you were sure you couldn't do it. But good news is that you did it. So, firstly well done for the same. And not taking more of your time best of luck for tomorrow. So enjoy.'

Gradually, the atmosphere became more dynamic. Shweta started singing and everyone joined in gustily on the last verse of her song.

By the crackling light of bonfire, Sandeep watched both Dhruv and Anjali had been nearly silent during the program over there. He couldn't remember the last time he had seen Dhruv so relaxed and happy on this trip. He didn't know what they were thinking, but he was very well consumed by the images from the scene at Darwa Top. He could still hear Dhruv's voice gently proposing Anjali. He knew that he had made a big deal with Dhruv's love but there was nothing he could do to fix it now. He could only hope for Anjali's '*Yes*' or mightbe Anjali would propose Dhruv before he proposes her.

Well, whatever will happen, let's leave on tomorrow – the only option Sandeep actually had left with.

The whole night, both Dhruv and Anjali couldn't sleep. Perhaps their eyes were busy in seeing beautiful dreams. Though there were some more also awakened till late night, but the reason for them was different. They were shivering like crazy even inside the down filled sleeping bags. It was the bone chilling cold and so everyone was desperately waiting for morning to happen.

None of them thought about it.

All three agreed to it – Amandeep, Namit and Nishit.

They could think of nothing better, and clearly they had to do something. They felt compelled to at least try, to do their best and make it work.

Early morning, still dark, almost murdering cold, the voice of three idiots in tipsy manner could be heard singing a song from movie '*Rang De Basanti*' continuously and gradually it seemed to be decreased. They crossed the lawn to the far side and stood looking out over the dark lake.

They heard footsteps on the path. Turned, stepped apart – appearing as cool as they wished. Dhruv was there rubbing his eyes.

'Hey Dhruv.' Nishit said.

'Hi. So, guys what's going on?'

'Nothing. Just fighting with this cold,' Amandeep said steadfastly with a smile.

And all started laughing.

They roamed in the lawn, to the rest of the area, and then sat at the end of the lake far from their campsite until the sun rays spread over the place.

Darwa top was around 5 km from the Dodital and at around 13,500 ft., a very tough climb as compared to the easy walk of last two days. The entire walk was an uphill climb. It starts with the climb along the feeder to Dodital breaking in to a thick birch forest opening into high meadows. Shepherds till today, graze their sheep and cattle in its lush green meadows. However, slowly, vegetation starts disappearing due to decrease in oxygen level. Sun's rays were very effective at this height. It seemed like your face will get burnt, so wearing goggles was not a fashion, but a need here.

Definitely, for all, with every difficult step to the fore, excitement to reach the target was also escalating.

One glance at Dhruv's face was enough to judge his state. Though somewhere he still had his doubts, the fear of Anjali's response, but Sandeep's words had a good upshot on him. He was all over happy, excited to reach his final destination.

Whatever the case – he needed to reach there.

And Anjali she walked side by side very carefully, then on via the path through the woods. She didn't take any help. Though she also had some doubts regarding Sandeep's words but still some power from inside was motivating her. Yet despite of Dhruv's hand, she was very much aware he was with her. He, of course, was the first person she'd actually wanted to meet on the top. Given the nature of the subject, given he was so much darling to her, she'd expected to feel some degree of . . . not shyness, but uncertainty when alone with him. When close to him.

Instead all, she'd felt, she was safe, both now and throughout the day. Not necessarily completely comfortable but assuredly not distressed even. Mentally functioning, she kept her eyes down and walked steadily on. Aware of Dhruv was coming behind her.

Aware she drew comfort from his presence.

Progressively, they emerged onto the edge of the area, a stretch of path where cold chilly wind blew up from opposite side. Anjali lifted her face to the breeze. It was awesome to enjoy it at this level. Dhruv hadn't surprised to find her doing this. Last two days had worked well to increase her stamina. Any other girl would have been resting, recuperating from the exertion of the day. Not Anjali. Though she also gets tired, relaxed lots of time in the way, but according to Dhruv, she was the most energetic girl he knew.

He let his gaze sweep down, over her slim figure, down over the length of her long, long legs. Definitely a point in her favour.

Anjali was also watching him secretly with every aspect she could. Sometimes, she tried to show being tired, started strolling, paused until he joined her, and then walked on but slowly, brows drawn down. For one instant, Dhruv couldn't imagine what she meant.

Gradually, they moved further. It was 12,600 ft. and the site was known as '*Darwa Pass*'. The pass in the bygone days enabled people to cross over from Bhagirathi valley to Yamnotri valley for trade, marriages and for offering prayers at Yamnotri temple. The pass was actually the last milestone for the Darwa Top and this last push was actually a heavy snow plodding. Thinking it might be dangerous for Anjali, Dhruv decided to be with her.

The snow was around two feet and was all powder. It was the bone chilling cold and very tough to cross the snowy area. Where on one hand it was difficult to step in the snow, the Sun was like torturing.

Anjali was out of her depth. With Dhruv at his side, she'd thought she had at least a passing acquaintance. She turned, passed him a smile and headed on. Dhruv understood, followed her, ambling at the side of her, holding her hands.

'Where are your gloves?' Anjali was almost surprised.

'Lost.'

'Where?'

'No Idea.'

Anjali stared at him. She could analyze that it was not an easy job for him to carry her to the top.

'You don't worry. I will go on my own.'

'I have no problem, you just move on' and Dhruv continued. Knowing well whatever had been bothering her was still running through her mind. He let his steps move on.

Anjali could see that Dhruv's one hand, with which he was pushing them upwards, gone almost numb because of snow. Even he was having a hard time with his knee. Lifting her hand suitably, she placed her fingers properly in his. This supporting touch inspired Dhruv.

'Move slowly. We have no rush.' Anjali glanced at him, and then turned to continue along the path. Wherever she saw, it seemed, Dhruv was there. There was a grin on her face. Her smile eased Dhruv's path. He moved slowly. Again Mr Sood's tortoise story came into his mind and he smirked. He was in high spirits.

He wanted to stretch the moment with fear, he was unaware of his fate of love, but very well this couldn't go much long.

Dhruv and Anjali could see the top. There were some people who had already reached there, dancing, shouting, enjoying blissfully.

Anjali blushed again. She wanted to reach immediately. There was something on her face, in her heart that was making her shy. She had finally decided that whatever will be the result, she will definitely propose Dhruv. After all he was her love.

Dhruv was even ready for the same.

And Sandeep he was waiting for the same since last night.

It was about one in the noon, everyone reached the top. The place was very windy and cold. A wave of success could be seen on every face. Every eye was shining. It was unbelievable for many what they did. Nishit, Amandeep and Namit as per their custom again sipped whisky in secret. It was awesome to be there at the top. Having snap shots of victory seems good, and the case was same there.

Watching clouds so closely was really something wild. All over surrounded by high ranges of Himalayas, Bandarpunch, Swargarohini was just like a dream of all got fulfilled. Although, there was another dream shining in two eyes still left, but there was nothing to worry as whatever is written always happened and the same also happened that day….

It was when Dhruv led Anjali on the top, Anjali glanced at him.

'Thanks,' Anjali said.

Now the moment was upon him – them – although Dhruv knew what he needed to say, but he wasn't sure how to proceed. He glanced at her, met her widening eyes. Perhaps, Anjali could sense his thoughts, but instead of conforming anything, she went straight to the heart of things.

'What did you want to talk about?'

Dhruv abruptly ran into grab. 'No…Nothing,' he turned thoughtful.

No one said a word for a while. Dhruv faced her.

She watched, waited, curious…

Ignoring the constriction in his lungs, he drew breath, met her eyes again.

'You know, you are beautiful,' though the words came directly from his heart, but he scolded himself.

'Dhruv Gupta, be on point,' he said to himself.

Anjali blinked, and then stared at him again but with a little anger this time. 'I was right; he is really a big Idiot in small package. Actually when it came to Dhruv Gupta, anything was possible.'

Dhruv set his jaw. When Anjali continued to stare, dumbfounded, he said 'Actually, I want to say, you are a nice girl. Just take care and never cry.'

Anjali found her to be lost in the swirl. She knocked her head.

'But when did I cry?'

Dhruv was almost confused. He uttered the words with so uneasiness, that he found himself sensing like any non-sense.

'Okay. Okay.' He breathed in.

'Actually I want to tell you a story.'

'I think he is really MAD, here a girl is dying for him and he wants to be a story-teller,' thought came in Anjali's mind.

'Do you ever hear the story of an apple tree?' he continued

'Which one?' Anjali asked astonishingly.

'The Law of Seed.'

And as he said the words Anjali started laughing heavily. Her reaction almost confused him.

'What happen? Why are you laughing?' Dhruv got unbalanced for a while.

Anjali said nothing but continued laughing. Everyone could hear her, sense an ecstasy in her laugh. All came near them with a mark of uncertainty on their faces. Every eye was on Dhruv. He felt very much embarrassed. Almost bewildered, thought of his love to be joke for her, startled him.

He headed down and just moved on to have a place, some place where he could be alone. But as he stepped forward, Anjali sat there only, taking support of her left knee and held his hand. Dhruv's lips had thinned, his eyes had narrowed. He waited for a heartbeat.

Anjali looked at him... blinked. "Maybe I am not the first girl to propose any guy like sitting on a knee, but I am sure I am the first one to propose someone beloved at this 13,500 feet."

"Will you marry me please?" She returned brightly while giving Shubhi's letter back to him.

Epilogue

Epilogue

The French Philosopher, Andre Comte-Sponville, had said: It is love which keeps us alive, since it alone makes life loveable. It is love which saves; it is therefore love which must be saved.

And that day I actually lived the sayings. He was right.

Hearing those words from Anjali's mouth were almost dreamlike. I'd imagined this moment so many times that I almost couldn't believe it was happening. My heart leaped, my eyes watered, and a wave of delight passed through my body. I didn't know what else to say. I mean, it was the sort of moment when one expected oneself to rattle off some kind of poetry or something. But I had nothing to say....

I was almost entrapped in her eyes. I smiled wider than I'd ever smiled before as if my face were going to break into two pieces. I'd finally gotten what I wanted. At last I had her all to myself. I'd waited this for so long. I'd never been this happy as I was at that moment as I felt myself melting into her embrace. Now I understood the message of that Dream. This is what's right – Anjali and me together. So, I told her how I'd been in love with her since the first day we met. I told her that I love more than anything; I wanted her to fall in love with me. I slipped my fingers in to her. I remembered the way my heart had beat when I had seen her first time.

The moment was about me and Anjali, I told myself. *Forget Shubhi*. So, I just loosened the letter from my grip and it got lost into the depths of Himalayas, not sure where. There was Anjali, and there was me. Nothing and no one else existed.

Life was beginning anew, and this time I was going to do everything right. This after all, was the real. I had reached the last stop of my journey into my heart... and somehow I found it very beautiful. So, I issued a silent thanks to God and resting my chin on the top of Anjali's shoulder, I just sat down in a silence that was almost blessed.

Time again passed but not gradually; this time it seemed to be very swiftly. We trek down to Dodital, then to Bhebra again and at last back to camp, then boarded our bus, heartfelt goodbyes to all instructors rang through the air, the bus roared to life, leaving Himalayas this time, then hit the highway road, then the freeway, and then back to a life far, far away from Uttarkashi on the same polluted roads of Delhi, back in to the real world.

But the truth is that Uttarkashi was not far away from me. In fact, it couldn't be. It is with me and I am sure, it will always remain with me, in my memories, like breath in my lungs. I can never forget what it actually gifted me. I can never forget any of the moment I lived during the whole leadership program.

Especially the one...

When we were just ready to head towards our home and Anjali drew me to her and kissed on my cheeks, right there in open in front of the whole world. There started a fluttering inside me, as if a butterfly was trapped there; beating its wing against my rib cage. I felt myself start to melt. My cheeks flamed with excitement as I'd never been so happy for last many months. And then only, a drumming sound filled my ears.

Soon, I realised it was the sound of someone clapping. I pulled away and looked around. He was none other than

Sandeep. I just tried to avoid his look with a shy, and same was the case with Anjali as she headed down her brows.

'Sorry to disturb both of you,' Sandeep said with a smile. 'But do you think you'll be able to get along now that you will not fight anymore?' He continued.

'Sandeep *yaar*, you' though I felt little disturbed, but I grinned, as I was already aware of the fact what Sandeep had done for me. Anjali had already told me everything in the bus. He was really a bastard and somehow I had been lucky enough to find such a friend.

'Okay. Okay. I am going. But before that I just want to say you one thing'

'What?'

'That Love always finds its way but if you love someone, just say......'